Sta

Romantic Comedy

Sophia Kingston

Copyright © 2016 Sophia Kingston

All rights reserved.

No part of this publication may be copied, reproduced in any format, by any means, electronic or otherwise, without prior consent from the copyright owner and publisher of this book.

This is a work of fiction. All characters, names, places and events are the product of the author's imagination or used fictitiously and are not to be construed as real. Any resemblance to persons, living or dead, actual events, locales or organizations is entirely coincidental.

ISBN-10: 1530073901
ISBN-13: 978-1530073900

Connect with me on
https://www.facebook.com/sophiakingstonbooks/

And sign up for my **newsletter**

…..to get an email notification as soon as the next book is available. ***Don't miss a single installment of Sophia Kingston's captivating Stardoom series.***

Book Description

Hollywood sweetheart, Lauralie Shaw, is accustomed to getting what she wants, when she wants it. Her spoiled attitude and demanding ways are notorious among her employees, and all of them do their best to keep her happy.

All, that is, until her father employed Colton Dixon to fly her private jet.

Colton has no patience for Lauralie's attitude, and no intentions of giving her what she wants. And soon, all Lauralie wants is Colton himself.

1

OK! Patient. Be. Patient.

Count to ten.

Lauralie Shaw closed her eyes, and *One... Two... Thrreeee.......... Fouuurrrrrrr.................*

Her eyes flew open. *They said.... No, Somebody said.... No, let me see.... Who the hell said that?* Lauralie tapped her index finger lightly on her chin and thought for a moment. *Anyway, whoever that bloody person was said that if we count to ten, it would help to calm the nerves. It was supposed to help calm us down. I have tried so many bazillion times, but the thing is, the thing is —.* Lauralie shook her head. *OK, fine! I. Can't. Do. It. I, Lauralie Shaw, who is the world's —. OK, wait. Maybe not the world. I, Lauralie Shaw, who is America's most famous celebrity just can't bloody do it.* She scowled.

A horn blared suddenly. It startled Lauralie and she was brought back to the present. A crease formed between her beautifully-trimmed eyebrows. "Stupid driver!" She cursed under her breath, glanced at her watch impatiently and heaved a loud sigh.

Lauralie had gotten up earlier than usual this morning, hoping to miss the heavy morning traffic on her way to the airport. But instead of the short, uneventful ride she'd hoped for, she was now stuck on the highway. Cars were quickly piling up behind theirs with angry, impatient monsters *(just like me,*

Lauralie thought) behind the wheels.

Lauralie craned her neck toward the tinted window of the chauffeur-driven limousine she was traveling in to see what was causing the stupid jam. She bobbed her head up and down, forward and backward like a chicken. The only thing she didn't do that chickens do is to make clucking noises. She had to refrain herself from doing that.

And Lauralie saw it! Red and blue lights that belong to a police car were blinking like a Christmas tree in the not-too-far distance. Oh God! Was that an overturned semi-truck and an ambulance? Several cones were placed on the ground, cordoning off two lanes out of the four-lane highway where the truck had overturned, causing a bottle-neck. And this had caused the jam! All the cars were trying to squeeze through the two lanes to get past the accident zone. A policeman was directing the cars of the already blocked lanes to the other side of the 'free' road.

And as if it was not already bad enough, the drivers, *out of their curiosity*, literally stopped their cars, hogged the whole road as if it belonged to their grandfathers, to take in the scene of the accident.

"Oh, damn it! Come on, come on, move guys. It's none of your business. Just get your butts moving!" Lauralie muttered angrily under her breath. "This is not it. These drivers are just wasting other people's time. Don't they know that time is precious?" She growled, and willed herself to write in to the United States Department of Transportation to give suggestions. Who knows? Maybe the suggestions she's going to give could save the country millions of dollars! One day, they would thank Lauralie for it. And maybe present her with some kind of award. Ha! She would become a saint and an advocate for the people!

The truth was — Lauralie had never been patient with anything. Patience was never her strong suit. Being an only child of the country's most popular celebrity couple, she would always get whatever she wanted as soon as she asked for it. *Whatever.* Her parents had given her the world, but hadn't equipped her to live in it. To Lauralie's father, she would always be his little girl. He'd pat her head every time and say with the goofy grin of his, "You're the pearl of the house." Even until now that Lauralie turned twenty-three years old.

After ten minutes went by without moving, Lauralie pressed a button on the door. The glass that separated her from the driver lowered slowly. "Any idea how long this gonna take?" she snapped at the chauffeur, even though she didn't mean to be so snappy. To be fair, he's innocent, and there's nothing he could do about the slow- moving traffic. Well, blame it on the reckless truck driver who caused all this. "I have a tight schedule today."

Hank glanced at Lauralie through the rear-view mirror and shook his head. "No idea, Ms. Shaw," he said flatly. To give him credit, he had worked for the Shaws for the past twenty-two years. He was the most trusted aide in the Shaw household and was like a second father to Lauralie since she was little. He knew her tantrums and her every movement. Apart from her parents, Hank understood Lauralie the most. And hence, he was accustomed to her attitude. "That's a big mess up there. It's gonna take as long as it takes."

"Can't you turn around or something?"

"Well, I guess I could." Hank agreed patiently as always — with Lauralie, "but we'd be driving into oncoming traffic. The nearest exit is a mile behind us. I don't expect we'd make it that far."

Lauralie pouted and pulled a long face.

"Don't worry, Ms. Shaw," Hank assured. "You're not flying commercial. You have your private plane waiting for you however late you may be." A wide grin crossed his face. "Why don't I put the screen back up, and you can sit back and take a nap? You'd want to be well rested so that you can catch up with your father later this afternoon."

Lauralie eased a little. Good old Hank. He always made Lauralie feel better every time. She had to agree that a little nap sounded great. Her insides crunched. She felt horrible for snapping at him earlier.

"Wake me when we're on the move again. I'll want to tidy my hair and make-up before getting on the jet."

"Got it, Ms. Shaw." Hank winked before pressing a button to put the screen back up. The thing about Hank was that he didn't take offense easily. No matter what tantrums Lauralie threw, or how badly she behaved, Hank would still treat her with respect. He would still treat her like his own daughter. Of course, Lauralie would feel *very* guilty after every tantrum. Every time.

Lauralie sighed and lay down on the long, overstuffed bench seat on the left side of the limo. She closed her eyes and willed herself to sleep, but it never came. She tossed and turned on the bench seat for a few minutes before she closed her eyes again, and forced herself to count the bloody sheep.

Sophia Kingston

US TRANSPORTATION DEPT
6789 New Jersey
SE, Washington, DC

6 September 2014

Ms. Lauralie Shaw
8700 Santa Monica Blvd
Los Angeles, CA 90000

Dear Ms. Shaw,

Thank you for your letter of 1 September 2014.

I am sorry to hear about your plight and I agree with you that the bloody drivers need to get on with their lives. I also agree with you that time is money and time wasted can cost the country millions of dollars.

Thank you for your suggestions to ban these road-hogging drivers from driving for ten years, and I assure you that we are working our best to solve the problem.

To answer your questions, I love chocolates and I don't watch TV as I simply do not have the time. Hence, pardon me if I don't know a hot star like you. Maybe, you can send me a photo of yourself?

Yours Sincerely,
George Martin
US Transportation Dept

P.S. I love your shows by the way.

2

Sebastian Shaw sky-rocketed to fame in the mid 80s. His lead roles in action movies shot him to the top of the chart. When he accepted a role in a small, independent film, everyone was surprised. *"Have you heard.......?"* or *"Are you sure?"* or *"He's going to act in that film?"* Everyone was exclaiming to each other, with ghastly expressions: mouths hanged open, eyes popped open like a goldfish and hands to their mouths. It was as though acting in that film was the hugest sin known to mankind. Unexpectedly, in the following year, he received a Best Actor Oscar for his role in that particular *small* film. And that shut everyone up.

Sebastian brought his then-girlfriend-now-Lauralie's-mother, Lana Foster, to the Oscar awards ceremony. She was Hollywood's 'darling' at that time. She worked her way up on the stages of Broadway. She hit big-time when she was cast in a supporting role on a big-budget Hollywood musical where she stole the whole show. Everyone gaped at her performance. After that big break, she had cast in lead roles in many major blockbuster movies.

Lauralie was proud of being the daughter of Sebastian and Lana Shaw, to say the least. To put it simply, she's proud of them. They became one of the country's biggest obsessions. They were known as 'the golden couple'. You won't see one without the other. They were not embarrassed to show affections toward each other in public. The display of their affections had shown the media and the public that they were still very much deeply in love after so many years of marriage. They became the envy of every woman. Just two years ago, they were voted the best role model for married couples.

Lauralie adored her parents to bits, and was their biggest fan of all time. As their no. 1 fan, Lauralie kept boxes of newspaper clippings and magazines, all with their pictures on front pages, in her closet. She started collecting them since middle school. The more recent pictures were of Lauralie in various stages of childhood. Ha! To think that the media was even interested in her childhood. Whenever she felt sad or lonely, she would browse through these boxes. It was her only way to hold on to those times. Those happy times when her mother was still alive. And she'd feel close to her mother again.

Everything was going well for the Shaw family. They had what everyone could only hope for — the status, the popularity, the fame, and everything in between. Then tragedy struck. Lauralie still remembered that day. She was in high school when she received news that her mother was diagnosed with third-stage breast cancer, aka *death sentence*. Her knees buckled and she nearly fainted. Her best friend reached out just in time to catch hold of her. Suddenly, the world came to a complete stand still. The fast moving world froze at that moment. Lauralie had difficulty breathing. It was like air being sucked out of her lungs.

Following the news, Lana canceled all her filming engagements and took a long break to concentrate on battling the illness. After a few rounds of chemo, the cancer went into remission. She was in the clear for a few years until it struck again last year — this time with vengeance. Doctors believe that if the cancer came back the second time, there's basically no hope. Sebastian refused to believe that. He flew in world-renowned cancer specialists. No matter how much the cost, he would pay top dollar just to get Lana well. They held on to whatever glimmer of hopes they had left, but deep down, they feared the worst. In the end, Lana Shaw succumbed to her illness.

Sebastian and Lauralie were devastated by the loss. Now, they only had each other left. Being her emotional bank, Sebastian became more indulgent on Lauralie, seeing how her mother's death had affected her so badly. She was like a zombie, staring into space most of the day. She'd cry herself to sleep at night. (No use counting the stupid sheep.) And she would do the same thing the next day, and the next, and the next....

Sebastian was worried. He would check on Lauralie to make sure she didn't fall into depression. He was devastated and depressed, too. (Even a blind person could see that. OK. A blind person couldn't see, but *surely* he could sense it?) Though he didn't show outwardly, Lauralie knew his insides were crushing just by looking into those soulful eyes. For her sake, Sebastian had put on a strong front. He cried himself to sleep many nights, and his eyes would appear puffy the next day. Just like Lauralie's would. Through this ordeal, they had grown even closer than close.

Lauralie's eyes flung open. Unknowingly, she had drifted off to sleep. She *so* missed her mother terribly. Tears began to well up and make its way down the sides of her face into her ears. *Ugh!* She so hate the feeling of water creeping into her ears. Lauralie imagined a big, hairy spider crawling into her ears and shuddered. She sprang up and wiped away the tears. She glanced out of the window to see how far they'd gone. *What?* Lauralie blinked her eyes again. *This can't be serious? We've only moved an inch?* She rolled her eyes and slapped her forehead. Seriously, she gave up.

"Great," Lauralie let out a huge sigh. There was no point getting mad with the things one couldn't control, right? It would only put more wrinkles on the face. She pressed the button to lower the tinted glass again.

As if on cue, Hank eyed her through the rear-view mirror on hearing the buzz of the window being lowered. "Still not moving, Ms. Shaw... though it looks like they're just about to clear up the mess," he explained.

"That's okay, Hank. You're right. It'll take as long as it takes. I was thinking about stopping in at Holly's while I'm in Aspen. Would you like me to get you anything?" Holly's is a gourmet sweet shop where Hank used to take Lauralie to when she was a little child. It's her most favorite shop in the whole world till today.

Hank's face brightened and broke into a wide smile. His face cracked into pieces, especially around his eyes. Although he's aging and hair was graying, Hank felt *"as healthy as ever"* as he always said and showed off his muscles. Lauralie imagined him in his underwear, with his bulging muscles, and posing like a weight lifter. She stifled a rising giggle. Hank continued to accompany the Shaws wherever they go. He's very much like a part of the family. They would be lost without him. As top celebrities, they were constantly followed by paparazzi, and Hank had a way of losing the stalkers in traffic every single time. It's his secret sauce, or whatever it's called.

"I've had a craving for Holly's peanut butter

fudge." Hank winked.

"Consider it done." Lauralie winked back.

Good old Hank. He was like a second father to Lauralie, always protecting her.

Lauralie still remembered the day vividly — the day she had arrived late at Manchester Academy, an all-girls' boarding school on the East Coast. She had gone to school happily, eager to make many new best friends, and thought nobody knew who she was. She wanted to be like any other kids and not let people think that she *pulled strings* to get into the school just because she was some celebrities'kid. However, things didn't turn out this way.

They were supposed to arrive before breakfast and settle into the dorm. When Lauralie arrived in a car during lunch time (damn the traffic jam, just like today), two-thirds of the school had been on the lawn. A group of nasty-looking older girls marched toward her. She got out of the car and stood rooted to the ground. What followed caught her completely off-guard.

"You must be that Hollywood brat," the blonde-haired girl with buck teeth sneered. Her high-pitched voice was so loud that anyone could hear it from miles away. Lauralie's mind didn't register her words; all the while, she was looking at the girl's buck teeth protruding out of her mouth. When she talked, Lauralie could see spurts of saliva droplets shooting out toward her. Instinctively, she darted aside. With her buck teeth, Lauralie bet she had difficulty keeping the saliva behind her lips.

"Of course she is, Vivian. Who else would think they can just show up whenever they please, with no regard for the school schedule?" the chubby redhead, with fats hanging over her skirt and buttons threatening to burst open on her shirt, rolled her eyes and smirked.

Lauralie was taken aback by the harsh greetings and, most of all, amused by what she saw. Her dream of making lots of best friends sank into the bottom of the ocean — just like the *Titanic*. "We were late for the airport," Lauralie mumbled. "There was a lot of traffic —"

"Oh yeah?" the girls interrupted and smirked. By then, a crowd had formed around them to watch the 'show'. Girls, big and small, were whispering to each other, pointing and eyeing at Lauralie. They knew who she was. Lauralie felt humiliated. Anger rose within her. Her fists clenched at her sides.

"I bet there was," Vivian continued. "A long line of traffic... of people... who wanted to bow down and worship you just because you are the daughter of America's most popular celebrity," she smirk-laughed. "Well, not us!" She waved a hand in the air.

The other girls snickered and sneered.

Lauralie fought back tears. Just then, Hank appeared at her side after he finished unloading the luggage, and glared at the girls. They stopped laughing suddenly, turned and scrambled for their lives as if they were running away from a monster. They would have easily won first place in a race, because in a second, they were nowhere in sight. The crowd dispersed quickly. Hank took Lauralie's hand and led her into the school.

The encounter with Vivian and her friends had been Lauralie's first experience with people who weren't impressed with her or her parents. She had lasted out the year at Manchester, and then transferred to a much friendlier and more liberal boarding school in Northern California.

Lauralie smiled, remembering that Hank had sent her there as well. These memories made her feel guilty for snapping at him earlier. It wasn't his fault that the semi-truck had overturned.

Finally, the limo moved past the accident zone and began to make its way to the airport. Lauralie breathed a sigh of relief, fetched her make-up bag from her bag while Hank maneuvered through the dense L.A. traffic.

3

"Good morning, Ms. Shaw," Anna greeted Lauralie cheerfully as she stepped on board the jet. Unlike other days, there was an unusual air of excitement around her today that Lauralie couldn't wrap her head around. There were even sparkles in her eyes.

"Good morning, Anna. Sorry to keep you waiting." Lauralie glanced at Anna, her cousin, curiously. As a favor to her aunt, Lauralie's father had hired Anna to serve as her flight attendant whenever she traveled.

"No worries, Ms. Shaw." Anna grinned. "Gave me a chance to get to know the new pilot." Anna couldn't stop herself from grinning, and that silly grin of hers grew even wider than just now.

Shifting her eyes and gesturing toward the cockpit door, Anna whispered to Lauralie excitedly, "I told him I'd introduce him to you once you come on board."

So this was it. The new pilot. This was what caused Anna to be so excited. The morning traffic had annoyed Lauralie so much that she had totally forgotten her father had hired a new pilot — again. In recent years, new pilots would come and go every few months. Despite the high salary and generous perks that they would receive for being Lauralie's pilot, most had called it quits using family, or so they declared, as their number one reason.

During interviews, Sebastian was always upfront with potential ones; he would warn them of his daughter's frequent travels. For Lauralie, she'd want them to follow and stay with her wherever she was. What could be more convenient than having them by her side at her disposal? If she wanted to go Las Vegas to party, they were there to fly her over. To Paris for Fashion Week, they would be there. Or even to Thailand for a short break? Damn! They were freaking there too!

Most pilots thought they could handle the grueling schedule – and Lauralie and her tantrums (which woman wouldn't throw tantrums, right? Right!). But in the last five years, no one had lasted more than six months each. The longest serving pilot she had was five months long.

"So, you've talked to him?" Lauralie asked. "Does this one have a wife who is going to complain about his frequent travels and long absence after two months? Or four months? Any kids?" Lauralie rolled her eyes and folded her arms across her chest. Her folding-arms-posture pushed up her already full cleavage in the sexy plunging neckline dress as if her breasts were going to pop out.

"No, Ms. Shaw." Anna shook her head and grinned. "This new pilot is unattached. And I mean really UN-attached!" Focusing on the word 'UN', she chirped excitedly, swinging her hands wildly as she spoke. She was like some crazy girl fan squealing when her idol appeared. She continued, "Oh, I can't believe this — unattached. Oh my gosh! He is so F-R-E-A-K-I-N-G hot!" Anna felt the blush rising to her cheeks and fanned her face with her hands. "You've got to see for yourself." She grabbed Lauralie by the arms, turned her around and shoved her toward the cockpit door.

Lauralie turned around to face Anna. "Hush, Anna! He'll hear from inside," she said in a loud whisper, jabbing her thumb toward the cockpit door behind her.

"Oh, don't worry. The door is sound proof. He won't be able to hear us," Anna continued excitedly. "You know what? He loves to travel. He'll fit into your lifestyle and schedule perfectly… and maybe…… fit as more than your pilot as well," Anna teased and winked at Lauralie.

"Oh, *pull-lease* Anna. Shut up!" Lauralie rolled her eyes. Since Anna had just gotten married, she'd been urging Lauralie to do the same as if marriage was the solution to life; as if all marriages would end up a happily-ever-after fairy tale. At least this was what it seemed to the naive Anna. She failed to realize that once the honeymoon stage was over, she and her new husband had to work doubly hard to maintain the marriage. To Lauralie, that was too much to bear. Being in showbiz, she had seen too many divorces happening around her. Many of her famous couple friends calling it quits after a few short years. And she didn't want to lose her freedom by committing her life to some man. Just yet.

"I think you're perfect for each other, just like a perfect match made in heaven. Two beautiful beings made for each other." Anna had always been envious of Lauralie's beauty. Well, envious but not to the point of being jealous. Long, silky blonde hair, deep-set blue eyes, high-bridged nose, small pouty lips, smooth porcelain translucent skin — so perfect in every way. Her beauty was what every young girl, or even older women covet after. They'd be contented to have even just one percent of her beauty.

"I'm already two hours behind schedule," Lauralie snapped impatiently. "Introduce me to the pilot so we can get off the ground. Go, get him and bring him out here. I don't want to be cramped in that small cockpit."

Anna's excitement died instantly. Lauralie's change of tone sent her scurrying into the cockpit to fetch the pilot. She reappeared moments later with a tall, muscular blonde man behind her. He was wearing the classic pilot's uniform — well-pressed collared short-sleeve white shirt and navy blue long pants, shiny black shoes that could mirror your reflection on them — looked like a lot of hours have been put in to polish them. To complete the pilot's look, a hat with the word 'Pilot' embroidered in the middle and something that looked like wings at each side of the word sat neatly atop his head. To add to his charming demeanor, he wore a pair of dark shades. He's totally hot. Just like what Anna said.

Anna glanced nervously at Colton and muttered, "Colton Dixon, this is Ms. Lauralie Shaw." Turning to Lauralie, "Ms. Shaw, this is Mr. Dixon."

Lauralie had worked with lots of hot hunks — actors and models. They were everywhere. But she had to agree with Anna, HE'S HOT. Nobody in the showbiz circle was as hot as this. He should become an actor. Snapping out of her thoughts, Lauralie demanded, "Take off those shades."

Anna was taken aback by Lauralie's harsh attitude toward Colton. Anna took a peep at Colton, praying very hard that he wouldn't react. If he did, he would be dead meat. Her gaze flicked to Lauralie and back to Colton again. She watched him carefully.

A smile lined his lips. Acceding to Lauralie's request, Colton lifted his hands and took off his sunglasses, much to Anna's relief. His piercing green eyes met Lauralie's. They're the most beautiful set of green eyes that Lauralie had ever seen. They were so mesmerizing that it sent shivers down her spine.

"Nice to meet you, Ms. Shaw." Colton held

out his hand toward Lauralie.

She snapped out of the trance and came crashing down to earth from on high — to the present moment. "Nice to meet you, Mr..... Dixon." Lauralie took his hand briefly and released. She cleared her throat and continued, "I do hope you can keep up with my schedule. Speaking of which, we're late. Let's get going, shall we?"

"We'll get moving as soon as we have an open runway," Colton said patiently.

"How long will that be?" Lauralie snapped. "I've never in my life waited for so long when I had somewhere to BE!"

"I understand you've had a stressful morning," Colton countered. "But snapping at me isn't going to help you with anything."

Anna's mouth dropped open as he spoke. No one had ever spoken to Lauralie like that before — not even her own parents. Anna looked in Lauralie's direction nervously to find her standing speechless, fingers clenched into fists hanging by her sides. Anna hoped in all hope that Colton would just shut up if he didn't want his face broken.

Having been warned of Lauralie's reputation by friends when they knew he's going to be Lauralie's pilot, Colton continued nonchalantly, "I've signed on to be your pilot, Ms. Shaw. I'm not your verbal punching bag. I can handle the long hours and being on-call twenty-four seven, but I will not be spoken to like I'm your inferior." He looked at Lauralie intensely. His green eyes appeared to be a shade darker than before. He looked so handsome. "If you can do that, we won't have any problems," Colton said suavely. "As I am the pilot, I am now going to return to the cockpit. I will let you know when we're cleared for takeoff. I hope you'll enjoy the flight. If you'd excuse me, please." He turned and retreated into the cockpit, without waiting for Lauralie's response.

Lauralie stood there, stunned. She opened her mouth but no words came out. She watched Colton's back as he disappeared into the cockpit. His words stung, but deep down, she felt a twinge of respect for him. No one had ever stood up to her like that before, to which she admired.

"Maybe I was wrong about him, Ms. Shaw," Anna said softly, one hand clasped over her mouth. "Maybe he's not gonna work out for you."

Lauralie composed herself after the shocking rebut. "It doesn't matter whether my pilot likes me or not. What's more important is that he comes when I call and flies the plane where I tell him to. That's all it matters." Eyelids became heavy, Lauralie yawned, "I'm going to lie down. Wake me twenty minutes before we land."

"Yes, Ms. Shaw." Anna nodded.

Like most things Lauralie owned, her jet was custom-made. She walked to the full-sized bed nestled in the rear of the cabin. She lay down on the bed thinking about her encounter and conflicted feelings with Colton. Anna was right; he was incredibly sexy. A jolt of excitement had shot through her body when he took off his sunglasses, revealing those mesmerizing eyes. But in a split second, her excitement had turned to fury by his words.

Lauralie sighed and closed her eyes. The last thing she wanted was to get worked up over a man who would probably be gone in a matter of months. She let herself drift off to sleep, eager to wake up in Aspen and start her day afresh. She hoped.

4

"Ms. Shaw? Ms. Shaw?" Anna called softly and tapped Lauralie lightly. Lauralie stirred and half-opened her eyes. "We're about twenty minutes from Sardy Field," Anna said.

"Thank you, Anna." Lauralie yawned sleepily. She sat up and stretched herself. She rose and walked toward her leather seat across the aisle. She retrieved her cosmetics bag and did a quick touch-up; though she still looked gorgeous even without makeup. She smoothed her hair with her hands.

Lauralie felt refreshed after her nap. She knew she wouldn't want her mood fouled again with another run in with Colton. She'd decided that as soon as the plane touched down, she would get off the plane immediately before Colton appeared.

Lauralie looked out of the window anxiously and she could see the runway looming nearer. The jet was just about to land. When the wheels touched the runway, the landing was so perfectly smooth. No jolts and jerks like what she'd experienced previously with her other pilots. She hated the 'horse-like ride' jerks — it made her giddy and nauseous.

Despite her unpleasant encounter with Colton earlier, the one thing Lauralie couldn't deny was the fact that his skills at handling the plane were perfect. *Perfect just like him.* Lauralie thought to herself. Her mind wandered off to those charming eyes and sexy lips. What would it be like to kiss those supple lips? It must feel soft. She mused. She imagined herself and Colton kissing passionately, sweaty bodies pressed hard against each other and hands roaming wildly. Her heart began to pound like crazy and she felt a tingling sensation all over her body at the thought.

The plane came to a halt. As if awaken from a trance suddenly, Lauralie inner-slapped herself and snapped out of her lustful thoughts. *How could you even think of that?* She scolded herself. It would never happen. Her blood boiled at the thought of the unpleasant exchanges with Colton this morning. She grabbed her bag and hurried off the jet before he could emerge from the cockpit.

A red Land Rover, which Sebastian had prepared on her arrival, greeted Lauralie once she emerged from the terminal. Her crew was already starting to load her luggage into the back seat of the car. She marched hastily toward the car and slid behind the wheel.

As Lauralie was waiting for the crew to finish loading her bags, she saw Colton coming out of the terminal and disappeared into the crowd. For a brief moment, Lauralie wondered how he would spend his weekend, who he would meet. *That's none of your business*, she scolded herself again. She shook her head hard, determined to shake away all thoughts of him from her mind. All of it.

A tap on the window startled her. It was the crew giving his okay. They had finished loading all her bags onto the car. Lauralie gave a faint smile and drove off.

Lauralie was excited to see her father. She'd been looking forward to this day. While Sebastian had made some good and bad choices in his personal life, he had made wise ones with his career. After winning his first Oscar, he abandoned action movies completely and focused on well-written, character driven scripts.

Sebastian began directing and started his own production company when Lauralie was five. He continued to act, but was able to be selective about the roles he cast in. Unlike many actors whose fame and wealth dwindled with age, Sebastian's didn't. In fact, he became even more famous and wealthy than before, much to everyone's surprise. Not even Lauralie knew how much wealth he'd accumulated over the years. She only knew that she'd never have to worry about money. They had plenty.

In true big Hollywood fashion, Sebastian became a philanthropist as he gained more money and status. Shortly after Lana's death last year, he founded a non-profit organization, Lana Shaw Foundation, which was dedicated to breast cancer research in her honor. It had outreach programs that provided free mammograms and counseling for lower income women who had breast cancer. The foundation was the reason why Lauralie and her father were meeting in Aspen. Sebastian wanted to discuss her role in the organization.

Lauralie had taken over the role of official spokesperson for the foundation shortly after she graduated from college. The role fit in with her schedule nicely. As a spokesperson, she's required to promote the foundation wherever she was, whenever she had a chance. Because of her modeling and filming assignments, she'd always traveled anyway and promoting the foundation didn't affect her schedule at all. It was something that she could squeeze some 'air-time' into her engagements, and needn't put in any extra days or effort which was the reason why Lauralie didn't mind doing her part to help. If it required her to do more, she'd say no. But as for Sebastian, he thought otherwise. Anything that didn't require any extra effort on her part is not a worthy cause. He wanted her to do something more. Something extra.

Lauralie had no idea what her father could possibly need to talk to her about her role as a spokesperson. But she was happy to have the chance to spend time with him. They hadn't seen each other for what Lauralie thought was a long time because of both their busy schedules. She missed him. She hoped that their get-together this time wouldn't be consumed with all business talk.

She smiled and sped off to the vacation home where her father was waiting.

5

Lauralie pulled up on the long driveway of their vacation home after a long drive. With reading glasses sitting on the bridge of his nose, Sebastian was seated on a couch at the porch reading newspaper. He lifted his head when the car turned into the driveway. He broke into a wide grin and rose from the couch when he recognized the red car.

The Land Rover came to a stop. Lauralie climbed out of the car and waved excitedly. She shut the door and ran toward her father like a little girl as he stretched out his arms to welcome her.

"Hey, darlin'." Sebastian burst into fits of laughter as he hugged Lauralie tightly. Regardless of how old she'd grown, in his eyes, she'd always be his little girl — the daddy's little girl. He stroked her hair gently and asked, "How was your flight? What do you think of your new pilot?"

Bloody pilot! For a brief second, anger flashed across Lauralie's eyes as she thought of the unhappy encounter with Colton. She gave a nonchalant shrug. She lifted her face and studied Sebastian. It's been a long time since she last saw him. He'd aged a little since her mother died — there were little cobwebs at both corners of his eyes and gray streaks appeared at both sides of his hair just above the ears. He'd taken a long break from filming and came to their vacation chalet at Aspen to get over his wife's death and to gain a new perspective on his life and career at the same time.

After a short pause, an evil grin lined her lips. "We'll just have to wait and see if he can keep up with me." Lauralie smirked.

Sebastian laughed so heartily that his shoulders shook. "My little jet-setter," he teased. "I'm glad you could take time out of your busy schedule to spend the weekend with an old chap."

"No, Daddy... You're not old at all. You're as young as before." Lauralie held onto Sebastian tightly as if he's going to disappear any minute. "I've missed you. And honestly, I could use a relaxing weekend in the mountains."

"Great to hear." Sebastian grinned. "But I'm guessing relaxing doesn't involve skiing?" Lauralie loved Aspen, but she hated skiing. Skiing is one sport that she'd never get a hold on. She would always tumble down the slopes and ended up looking like a fool, with her ski poles flying everywhere. And it's so damn difficult to get up once you're on your ass. To make things worse, winter only happens a quarter out of the entire year, and hence it didn't give her the time she'd like to master this sport.

"I don't want to go skiing, Daddy. But you should since you love it." On the other hand, skiing was Sebastian's favorite winter sport. He was an expert and he's able to slide across from one end to the other end of the mountain in a zigzag fashion like a professional. Much to the envy of Lauralie. And no matter how much Sebastian taught and guided Lauralie, skiing was just not for her. And she gave up.

"You won't mind me leaving for the slopes for a few hours tomorrow?" Sebastian asked.

"Of course not. Maybe I'll see if Stella can fit me in for a beauty day."

"I've already made you an appointment." Sebastian smiled. "I know my girl. I booked you the Premium Package, starting at eleven in the morning. I thought you might want to sleep in after your long day of traveling."

"Thank you, Daddy!" Lauralie shrieked excitedly and gave a peck on his cheek. Sebastian always knew what she wanted.

"Let's get inside, it's freezing out here." Sebastian put his arm around Lauralie as they made their way into the house. "I have a fire going, lunch ready, and dinner is already roasting in the oven."

The aroma of roasted chicken greeted them as they stepped into the house. Fire was dancing wildly in the stone fireplace at the far corner, and Beatles music played softly in the background. Lauralie closed her eyes and basked in the aroma.

When Lauralie was little, her parents had employed a full staff of maids, butlers, and personal chefs, so they never had to do the cooking and house chores themselves. But when they visited one of their vacation homes, the Shaws would always do everything themselves, including cooking. It was just too much trouble to hire temporary helpers, and wasteful to permanently staff a whole house when the Shaws were only there for a short time.

Sebastian had always been a good cook and Lauralie enjoyed every single dish that he'd dished out. "It's the best in America!" Lauralie would always say.

"Oh.. That smells so good!" Lauralie exclaimed excitedly. She walked over to a bar stool at the kitchen island and sat down.

"There's a cheese sandwich over there if you want a quick bite while I prepare the table," Sebastian said, pointing to the neatly wrapped sandwich on the dining table across the kitchen. "You must be hungry."

Just then, Lauralie's stomach growled. She was indeed famished. She hadn't realized how hungry she was until now that Sebastian had mentioned. And even more so because of the aroma of the roasted chicken. She had not eaten anything as she'd slept through her entire flight. She hopped over to the dining table, grabbed the sandwich and gobbled it down as if she hadn't eaten for days.

"Woah.. Slow down, honey." Sebastian

chuckled, glancing at her while placing the plates on the dining table.

"I'm dying of hunger, Dad." Lauralie stuffed the rest of the sandwich into her mouth. "I haven't had anything since morning."

"Well.. Well.. Look at the way you eat." Sebastian laughed. "I thought you haven't eaten for days!" Sebastian glanced at Lauralie. "Al...right, lunch's ready," he said as he placed the last dish — honey-combed chicken wings — on the table.

Lauralie hopped over to the table, eager to see what her dad had cooked. Sebastian would always cook her favorite dishes. "Yum! Yum! Honey-combed chicken wings and...... black pepper rib-eyed steak! My favorites!" She rubbed her hands together. "Thanks, Daddy." She gave Sebastian a bear hug.

"Come on, let's tuck in. I'm hungry." Sebastian pulled out a chair for Lauralie. He then walked over to the opposite side of the table and sat down.

Lauralie took a bite of the honey-combed chicken wing. The juice flowed out as her teeth sank in. "Hmm.... it tastes so good.." Lauralie closed her eyes and commented, as if she's on drugs.

"It's the best in America," both Sebastian and Lauralie said in unison, and then broke out in laughter.

"Oh.. Daddy." Lauralie giggled and reached

out for another wing.

"That's what you would always say." Sebastian laughed heartily. "I know my girl."

"I know my girl," Lauralie said in a manly voice, mimicking her father.

They laughed. They devoured their meals in silence for a moment before Sebastian spoke again.

"Lauralie," Sebastian said in a more serious tone, "it's time you take a more serious role in the foundation."

Lauralie almost choked at his comment. She reached for the glass of orange juice and washed the steak down her throat with it, and put the fork of rib-eyed steak down on her plate. She looked at him, eyes wide opened. "What do you mean by a more serious role?" she asked. "I spent all of my time traveling and talking about the foundation as a spokesperson. You mean I'm not serious enough after all I've done?" She lifted the fork and yanked the steak out into her mouth.

"Yes, I know Lauralie." Sebastian placed his hand over hers. "You talked about the foundation a lot... in St. Thomas, at the Met Gala, during Fashion Week... but all of these places are places you wanted to go anyway," he said, looking at her with tender eyes. "But what I want for the foundation — for you as a spokesperson — is to visit an outreach center and speak to children who are suffering real losses. And not to promote the foundation to people who don't understand the pain at all. That would be more meaningful."

"But these people donated money, don't they?" Lauralie argued. "As long as we can get the donations and it goes to the outreach centers and the suffering children, what's the problem?" She poked at a few strands of fries angrily with the fork and stuffed them into her mouth.

"Yes, but I would think that you'd want to do more... I want you to live a life of more substance and meaning."

"What do you mean.. a life of more substance?" Lauralie was losing her patience.

"Honey, I'm an old man, and I have more than my share of regrets. First and foremost is the regret that I raised you without any clue as to what the real world is like. I wanted to protect you, to make you happy. But as I've gotten older, I've realized that I never taught you what's really important... because I'd never realized what was important myself. We've had a blessed life, Lauralie, even with the loss of your mother. We've been blessed, and it's time we both give more back."

"So what exactly do you want me to do?" Lauralie dropped the fork on the plate and folded her arms across her chest. "Quit showbiz, work in the foundation and disappear from the public eye?"

"No, that's not what I mean, Honey," Sebastian clarified. "I don't want you to stop raising funds for the foundation. I just want you to do more outreaches when you're home or traveling. I've discussed it with Rachel, and she's putting you on the schedule as a lead speaker at a family counseling session in L.A on Thursday night. When you travel from now on, you will be scheduled to speak at a cancer support center nearby."

"And if I say no?" Lauralie challenged, lowering her eyes to her plate on the table. The thought of public speaking made her nervous. It's not that she's not used to appearing in public — she's a celebrity who appeared in shows after all — where all is glamour. But having to speak to people about her struggles and sufferings is just not her — especially in outreach centers. It would be too emotional for her. She still missed her mother since her death — a lot.

"If you say no, I'll just leave it as that," Sebastian conceded. "But I'd like you to consider it — for me, Lauralie. I haven't asked anything of you before until now, have I?" His voice was barely audible.

Lauralie knew he had a point. She'd always been allowed to do what she wanted. She'd had more than her fair share of dramatic, public break-ups that filled the tabloids for months at a time. As with any other teenagers, she'd had her rebellious side. She'd been arrested twice in college — once for shoplifting and once for driving under the influence. And her parents had never once lectured her about it. Sebastian made sure she was alright, and never told her to 'shape-up' or accused her of damaging the family's reputation. Lauralie knew she'd had it all too easy. She felt guilty for snapping at her father earlier.

After a long pause, Lauralie nodded and gave Sebastian a weak smile. "I'll think about it, Daddy."

"Thank you, Darling. That's all I'm asking." Sebastian broke into a wide grin and stood up. "Now, what would you like me to make for dessert?"

6

Lauralie woke early the next morning, way before her alarm went off. This was unusual for her as she would always have difficulty waking up in the mornings. Though tired, she did not have a good sleep. She had been tossing and turning in bed with intermittent sleep.

Lauralie looked out of the window. The sky was just beginning to brighten up. At the look of it, it should be around six-thirty to seven o'clock. She reached out for the alarm clock on the side table and peeped at it. Seven o'clock. It would be another four hours before her spa appointment at eleven.

She brought her arm over her forehead. She stayed in bed and stared at the ceiling above her. A thousand and one things ran through her mind. She thought about what her father had said the day before and her encounter with the pilot — her conflicted feelings toward Colton.

Pointing out her shallowness seemed to be the running theme this weekend. Lauralie was happy with her life and didn't think speaking to cancer patients and their families would bring her any more joy. She'd promised her father she'd think about it just to appease him. She loved him too much to see him disappointed. When she's back in L.A., she'd find reasons — or excuses rather — to not visit the outreach center.

The alarm sounded and she jerked up. At one point, she had drifted off to sleep. With a loud yawn, she got out of bed. She showered quickly, patted herself dry and picked up a pair of stretchy yoga pants and an over-sized designer sweatshirt. She swooped her hair in one sweep and bundled it. Five minutes later, she was out of the house, on her way to the spa.

* * *

"Good day, Ms. Shaw. How are you? Hope you're doing well," a tall brunette greeted her warmly as she stepped into Stella's.

"I'm great, Amanda," Lauralie answered.

"Good to hear that, Ms. Shaw." Amanda gave Lauralie a wide grin. "Come, follow me." Amanda gestured with her hand, turned and walked toward a private room. Lauralie followed her. Stella's was a popular spa among celebrity guests, and they prided themselves in providing privacy and excellent customer service.

Lauralie loved to come to Stella's whenever she's in Aspen. The ninety-minute massage always made her feel so relaxed that all her tiredness and tensions were forgotten. Just the sweet and spicy scent that hung in the air alone was enough to make her forget all her troubles. It felt like hiding in a safe haven. She'd hoped that the unpleasant events that happened these few days would be thrown far back somewhere behind her brain.

Lauralie went into the changing room. She undressed and wrapped herself with a towel that Amanda handed her earlier. She marched to the familiar spacious massage bed at the far end that was reserved for her use. With soothing music in the background, Amanda began working skillfully on her body with essential oils. The essential oils smelt so good and therapeutic that Lauralie eventually drifted off to a faraway land.

* * *

"Ms. Shaw? Ms. Shaw?" Someone patted Lauralie on the shoulder gently. Lauralie stirred and struggled to open her eyes. It was Amanda. Smiling, she said, "All done with massage, Ms. Shaw. Now on to facial."

With Amanda's help, Lauralie turned over, facing up. Amanda began to massage gently on her face with cleanser. After facial, Lauralie was whisked off to another room for the last session of the day — manicure and pedicure. Her nail technician was none other than the spa owner, Stella, herself. Stella had taken a liking to Lauralie as a child and would always do her nails personally.

"You look great, Stella," Lauralie commented as the older lady settled into a chair opposite hers. Stella took her hands and began to work on her fingernails.

"Thank you." Stella looked at Lauralie and beamed from ear to ear — so wide that Lauralie thought her face would crack anytime. Stella stopped buffing her nails for a moment and raised her left hand to show off a diamond ring on her ring finger.

"Oh my God!" Lauralie held her hand and stared hard at the ring with wide eyes. "Congratulations!" She looked up at Stella and back at the ring again. "But I thought you and Steve are happy with the way things are and had decided not to make it official?" Stella had always been an independent woman and had insisted that she wouldn't want to go through all the hassles of getting married. She was happy with her status quo.

Stella giggled like a little girl. "Well, it's necessary now," Stella explained as she continued to buff her nails. "Steve and I want to have a child. But because I'm too old, I can't carry one. We've decided to adopt and we'll have a much better chance if we're legally married."

"Too old?" Lauralie looked at Stella with puzzled eyes. "I thought you're only thirty-eight!" To Lauralie, that's not old. Mid-forties was.

Stella laughed. "I am indeed thirty-eight. And

according to my doctor, that's too old. Steve and I have been trying for the last year. I actually thought I was pregnant, so I went to the doctor. And found out I wasn't pregnant, I have early onset menopause."

"Oh." Lauralie didn't know what to say. She lowered her gaze to her nails which Stella was furiously buffing. "I'm sorry." Any woman who couldn't fall pregnant to have their own biological children would be upset.

"That's okay, sweetheart." Stella glanced at Lauralie briefly. "Maybe that's the way it's meant to be. That's what Steve and I tell each other. We were upset and depressed at first, but we've got over that stage. Our child is out there somewhere, or will be soon. And I can't wait. It was my fault that I hit the snooze button on my biological clock for so long while I built up this spa business." Stella lifted her gaze and looked around the place with pride. It was what it was now because of years of dedication and hard work she had put in. Her gaze met Lauralie's and continued, "Now that the business is successful, all I want is to be someone's mom." Stella laughed, shaking her head as though it's unbelievable to begin with. She lowered her gaze and continued to work on Lauralie's nails.

Lauralie looked at Stella for a moment. Stella had always been her role-model. Like Lauralie, she was raised by Hollywood parents — her mom an actress and dad, a stuntman. Both had similar childhoods, but Stella was never interested in showbiz and thus had shied away from the Hollywood scene.

Owning a spa had always been Stella's childhood dream. After she graduated from business studies, it was no surprise that Stella used her trust fund to start up the spa business — to much fanfare. Many famous celebrities turned up to witness the opening ceremony, and they became her long-time customers ever since. Stella was the epitome of an independent, successful career woman.

After building up a wildly successful spa business, Lauralie was surprised when Stella now longed for a common life — to get married and start a family. Everyone seemed to have some regrets at some point in life which led to a change in what transpired. She thought about what her father had said the previous night — about his regrets as he got older. And now Stella — her regrets of not starting a family earlier.

"All done." Stella broke into Lauralie's thoughts and brought her back to the present. She looked at Lauralie and smiled as she screwed the cover back on to the nail-polish bottle.

Lauralie glanced at her nails and wriggled her fingers. "Thanks. Nice work." She admired as she stood up. "I'll see you around. Send my regards to Steve." She smiled and headed toward the door, thinking about her own regrets, if there were any. None, she hoped.

7

Lauralie glanced at her watch. It was two in the afternoon after a good and relaxing spa treatment at Stella's. She decided to drive to Aspen's quaint shopping district as she knew her father wouldn't leave the slopes until nightfall.

Other than her mother, skiing had been Sebastian's other love since the beginning. No matter how busy he was, he would always come to Aspen for up to at least a week to ski during the winters. It was his way of de-stressing as he always said.

Lauralie pulled the Land Rover into a parking lot. She slipped five dollars into the payment box and headed toward the shopping mall. As she was walking, she spotted a familiar figure walking toward her in the opposite direction. Her heart skipped a beat. Who could be in Aspen other than...? She slowed down to a halt and squinted her eyes in the hope to see clearer. When the figure came nearer, her breath got caught in her throat that she almost stopped breathing and needed an oxygen tank. She'd guessed correctly — it was Colton.

Lauralie's heart was beating so hard and fast that it was threatening to explode. She didn't know what to do and was unable to move as if she was stuck to the ground. Colton was moving closer and closer toward her. She had to think fast. She had two options. She could change her course of direction by walking to the other side of the street. Or she could pretend not to notice him by fidgeting on her phone — pretending to call or SMS someone. But she can't. It was too late by the time she decided on the latter. He was standing right in front of her, grinning.

"Hello, Ms. Shaw," Colton greeted. The incident in the jet yesterday seemed to not bother him that much like how it had bothered Lauralie. Whatever that had happened between them seemed to have dissipated into thin air. Well, at least to him.

"He.. Hello." The sight of him still gave Lauralie flutters in the stomach. As much as Lauralie tried to calm her nerves, she felt her cheeks blushing. She hoped Colton wouldn't notice. "I'm surprised to see you here." Lauralie squeaked — her voice a notch higher than she intended to. And the words tumbled out of her mouth like waterfall before she could stop them.

"Well, I'm *not* surprised to see you here," Colton responded and grinned.

What? Lauralie fumed and she shot daggers at him.

Colton raised his hands as a sign of surrender. "Woah, I'm just kidding. Cool." He seemed to have softened somewhat compared to the previous day; his words friendlier instead of condescending. Lauralie felt stupid for reacting the way she had and gave him a smile that seemed to be plastered on her face. He held up a small shopping bag. "I needed to buy a gift and that's why I'm here," he explained.

"Is that a buy-off for the woman you left at home?" Lauralie asked, glancing at the shopping bag. Was there a tinge of jealousy in her tone? If there was, she sure hoped Colton wouldn't take notice.

Colton raised his eyebrows, taken aback by her question. He shook his head and chuckled. "No, no.. it's a birthday present for my niece. She turns fifteen next week. Think she'll like this?" He pulled out a soft cashmere sweater from the bag.

Lauralie paused for a moment. Why was she feeling a sense of relief when he said the gift was for his niece?

"Oh.. ya.. yes. If she has good taste, she'll love it." Lauralie laughed nervously. As they continued to talk, she felt more comfortable and at ease with Colton. "Are you enjoying Aspen so far?"

"This is my first time here." Colton looked around before fixing his eyes back to Lauralie. "So far so good. Heard Aspen is a great place for skiing. A regret I've never learned how to ski when I was little." He sighed. After a short pause, he continued, "I was about to find somewhere for lunch. Any good eats around here?"

"There's a place I'd go to whenever I'm here. It has some of the best foods. It's a ten-minute drive from here." Lauralie paused. "I was thinking of having lunch myself. Would you mind some company?"

"Of course I don't mind. We both have to eat anyway."

"We can take my car," Lauralie offered.

Colton agreed and followed Lauralie to where her Land Rover was parked. They climbed into the car and drove out of the tourist section of Aspen. With music playing from the car audio, they drove in silence until they arrived in a small, modest residential area.

"Here it is." Lauralie turned into a small lane and pointed to a small café at the corner of the street.

Colton's gaze followed the direction where her finger pointed. Looking in from outside, the café was small and homely. It's bustling with activity; it was almost fully packed, waiters and waitresses taking orders and scurrying around serving up dishes.

"Where is this place?" Colton glanced around. He was surprised by the humble setting of this small café. Instead of a posh, five star restaurant he'd expected Lauralie to bring him to, she had brought him to this modest café nestled in this lesser-known small town.

"This is the best place to eat in. Their food is the best in Aspen," Lauralie said as they pulled into an empty parking lot in front of the café. "This place is always packed though it's a lesser-known place. Their food is that good!" Lauralie jacked up her thumb to show a good sign and glanced briefly at Colton.

Colton smiled.

The Lauralie today was a completely different person as compared to the Lauralie he first met in the jet yesterday; the sweet and kind version versus the arrogant, bad-tempered, and impatient version. He saw two different sides of her in just a day. He wasn't surprised at how she'd treated him yesterday in the plane; he'd heard so much bad press about her before he became her pilot.

She isn't so bad after all, Colton thought. He looked at her for a long while. *Beautiful, checked. All the curves in the right places, checked. Temper, still a work-in-progress. If she could be sweet and kind just like today, she'd be perfect.*

Colton was attracted to her, without him realizing it.

8

The bell chimed as they entered through the glass door of the café. Laughter and chattering filled the air.

"Hello, Ms. Shaw. It's lovely to see you again!" A small, older man greeted them as he came round from behind the counter. "How is your father?"

Several tables of people lifted their gazes and glanced in their direction. They whispered among themselves; they recognized Lauralie. However, she didn't bother with the attention. She'd grown accustomed to it as a public figure.

"It's great to see you too, Ernesto. My dad's doing well. He's on the slopes skiing right now." Lauralie chuckled. "Meet my friend, Colton Dixon." Turning to Colton, she introduced, "Ernesto Garcia, the owner and head chef here at the café."

"It's very nice to meet you," Colton greeted, extending his hands, which Ernesto took.

"Nice to meet you too," Ernesto returned the greeting, nodding his head slightly.

Ernesto led them to Lauralie's favorite booth at the back of the café. "Would you two like to take a look at today's menu?" he asked once they're seated.

"I don't need to, Ernesto. Just bring me my usual medium-rare beef steak." Lauralie smiled. She had always ordered it whenever she was here since as long as she could remember. It was her favorite among the many dishes.

"That sounds good. I'll have that as well," Colton said, glancing at Ernesto.

"Got it. We'll serve you shortly." Ernesto turned and disappeared into the kitchen.

Colton looked around the cafe. Dimly lit and lined with brick walls all around, the café logo that read ERNESTO'S was decorated in the center of the wall where the counter stood. Two spotlights shone on the logo at each side. A few pictures of the café's food — the Chef's recommendations — were scattered around the walls. On the wall to the left of the counter was a good-sized rectangular chalkboard with hand-written menu. It added a homely touch to the already homely café.

Taking in the simple-decorated cafe, Colton said with a tone of admiration, "Well, well, I'm surprised." He raised an eyebrow and fixed his gaze on Lauralie which made her a tad uncomfortable. His beautiful eyes appeared to be greener than before. "I thought you'd pick somewhere swanky, full of vegan food and *pretentious* people." He gestured with his fingers in quotes when he said the word pretentious.

Lauralie rolled her eyes. "Don't judge a book by its cover, okay? And for your information, I think vegan food is disgusting." She cringed and made a face at Colton.

Colton snort-laughed. "Looks like we've finally found something we agree on," he joked. "But seriously, this is a surprise... a pleasant one."

"Ernesto is my dad's childhood friend," Lauralie said. "We've been coming here since I was little." She smiled, remembering fondly the happier times when they'd come here together as a family. Together with her mother when she was still alive.

Just then, a waitress — Wendy as written on her name tag — appeared with a bottle of sparkling water and an assortment of cheeses, dips, and freshly baked crackers.

"Careful with the crackers, just pulled them out from the oven," Wendy said as she laid them carefully on the table. "Your beef steak will be out shortly."

"Thank you." Lauralie smiled.

Wendy smiled and returned to the kitchen.

Colton took a bite of the cracker.

"Hmm... this is delicious," Colton conceded after eating the herb cracker topped with fresh goat cheese.

"Wait till you savor the steak."

"I don't know if I'll have room for the steak." Colton laughed, gesturing at the spread before them. Ernesto had always served the Shaws a generous serving of entrée.

"It won't matter. One bite of Ernesto's beef steak and you'll devour the whole plate in no time, room or no room." Lauralie eyed Colton mischievously.

After a few minutes, Ernesto appeared with two big pearly-white round plates. "Your beef steaks here," he announced. The juicy-looking beef steaks with crisscrossed lines in the middle were still sizzling hot; you could see white steam dancing atop the steaks. On each side of the steak was a generous serving of fries and greens, finished with dashes of red pepper powder at the sides of the plates as décor.

Ernesto set the plates down in front of them.

"Enjoy your steaks," Ernesto said.

"We will." Lauralie beamed and reached out for the fork and knife.

Ernesto returned to the kitchen.

"This looks delicious." Colton stared and salivated at the beef after Ernesto left. He sat upright with fork and knife already in his hands, ready to devour every inch of the steak. He looked like an excited child in a candy store.

The comical sight of him made Lauralie burst out laughing. *When did he take up the fork and spoon?*

She watched him as he sliced the steak and put a piece into his mouth.

"Hmm... this tastes heavenly." Colton closed his eyes as if he was in ecstasy as he put another sliced piece into his mouth.

    Lauralie chuckled.

    They ate in silence as they gobbled down their steaks like a predator devouring its prey.

9

"So, your favorite place to eat is this quiet little local joint here in Aspen?" Colton broke the silence as he gobbled down his last slice of steak, "And you're not afraid to chow down your food in front of people?" Colton cocked an eyebrow. He was amused at the sight of Lauralie gobbling down her steak like nobody's business earlier on. "You're just so full of surprises, Lauralie Shaw."

"You wouldn't be surprised at all," Lauralie countered, "if you hadn't already made up your mind about me." She drew an invisible circle in the air with the fork

."You're right... I admit I'm guilty of that." Colton put his hand to his heart. "I sincerely apologize."

"It's okay, I'm used to it." Lauralie sighed softly. "Everyone I meet already has their own idea of who I am — spoiled little rich girl, no substance, right? I've heard it since I was little."

"Well, you've developed a bit of that reputation in the press. That's the truth," Colton said softly.

"I was saddled with the reputation a long time ago," Lauralie rebutted, "and I spent many frustrating years trying to convince people that they're wrong about me. But nobody wanted to listen to me; to know the real me... no one at school, no one in Hollywood, and certainly, no one in the press." Lauralie sighed again and rubbed her temple with her fingers as if to ward off a headache. "So I gave up. I learned at a young age that people treat you better when you behave the way they expect you to, even if they expect you to behave badly."

"That must be a frustrating way to live," Colton said softly, loud enough for Lauralie to hear amidst the chatters and laughter around them.

Lauralie shrugged, resigned to fate. "It is what it is. I wouldn't trade my life for anything, even if I'm destined to be labeled by other people's assumptions. I'm happy where I am."

Colton felt a twinge of guilt for treating her so harshly the day before. Like others, he had a preconceived perception of her. That explained his harsh behavior toward her.

Just then, Wendy emerged from the kitchen with their dessert — bread pudding — and set it before them.

"Okay, enough about me." Lauralie took a sip of the sparkling water before starting on her dessert. "You knew all about me, or thought you did, before we ever met. I want to know more about you." Lauralie took a quick glance at Colton before focusing her attention back to her bread pudding. "Where did you grow up? What was your childhood like?"

Colton took a mouthful of the bread pudding before he began. "I was born in Michigan. My father worked at a Chevy factory, my mother worked for Ford. I knew I didn't want to work on the line, so I joined ROTC in high school, and left for the Air Force two days after I graduated high school."

"I didn't know you were in the military." Lauralie raised an eyebrow. "How many tours did you do?"

"Two." Colton paused before answering. "First Afghanistan, then Iraq."

"You're no longer in service? Were you injured?" Lauralie asked, assuming that was the reason he left.

Colton sat in silence for a long while. He stared into space — lost in his own thoughts, lost in his own world. He looked distant and what Lauralie thought was sadness in his eyes. Pain was written all over his face.

He met Lauralie's eyes and finally answered softly, "No, I wasn't injured... You've watched *Saving Private Ryan*, haven't you?"

His question tugged at Lauralie's heart. "You don't mean..." she gasped, clasping her hands together, hoping that her assumption was wrong.

"Unfortunately, yes. My younger brother, my only brother..." Colton's voice trailed off. His mouth remained open. He seemed to be speaking but words just didn't come out; they got stuck in his throat. He made some funny noises at the back of his throat.

He shifted his eyes to a spot on the table, and finally managed. "He followed in my footsteps and joined the military to get out of Michigan. We both thought we knew what we were doing... thought we'd serve our time and then go to college on the government's dime." Colton paused for a long while as if trying to compose himself, before he continued. "His plane was shot down on the third day of his first tour. The Air Force offered me an honorable discharge, and for my parents' sake, I took it. It's painful enough for them to lost one son and I don't want them to go through the pain of losing another, if it happens."

Colton closed his eyes and lowered his head. He ran his fingers through his hair and held his head as if in frustration. Pain and sorrow was etched all over his face.

The whole place fell silent suddenly — to Lauralie. She was stunned into silence. She didn't know how to react to Colton, and what's more, to comfort.

"I'm so sorry to hear that." Lauralie finally managed after a few more moments of silence. Her voice was so soft that it's barely audible. "I know how awful it is to lose someone you love."

Colton lifted up his head and looked at

Lauralie. The tip of his lips broke into a smile. "I know you do." He placed his arms on the table and leaned toward her. "I didn't mean to bring the mood down. This isn't a great dining conversation." He laughed uncomfortably.

Wendy returned to their table with two generous servings of vanilla and chocolate gelatos. "Your favorite gelatos, Ms. Shaw."

Lauralie thought she'd made a mistake. "We didn't order these."

"Ernesto said it's on the house," Wendy explained.

"That's wonderful! Thank you so much." Lauralie smiled. "We're on the same check, just bring it to me when you have a moment."

"I'll be right back." Wendy turned and walked toward the counter.

"This meal's on me," Colton said as he took a spoonful of the gelato.

"No, let me pay for it. I brought you here," Lauralie insisted. "The next time will be your treat."

Colton nodded and smiled. "Okay then. Thanks." He watched Lauralie as she ate the gelato. Her reputation had made him hesitate accepting the job as her pilot. It seemed now that the job would be nothing like he'd imagined. He had began to enjoy being with her.

10

His eyes flew open. A dream has woke Colton up and it made him feel uneasy. He dreamt of his torrid, dramatic romances with Lauralie and how it blew out of proportion in the tabloids nationwide. Their scandalous news were flashed across all channels — all newspapers, gossip magazines, and all other outlets they could ever find. And even on the internet.

Colton's ex-fiancé was obsessed with celebrity gossips. She would keep tabs on the latest gossips in the tabloids, and he would always get to know about them first-hand from her. He knew more than he'd ever wanted to know about Hollywood's most popular celebrity.

The year Lauralie turned eighteen, the Examiner had done a huge cover story, with the headline "SHE'S FINALLY LEGAL!!!". That edition broke sales records, and every magazine in the industry had tracked her relationships since then. According to reports to date, she'd been involved with the son of an angsty, independent film director, the lead singer of a heavy metal band, and most recently, her personal trainer, who was twenty years her senior.

Colton had been Lauralie's pilot for only two days, and he'd broken one of the promises he made to himself. He had sworn that he would keep a distance and not develop any interest in her, going into the job. Not to mention the fact that he had no desire to end up in one of those piece of shit tabloids.

But he broke it — yesterday.

You've already crossed the line, dickhead. Colton scolded himself and slapped the back of his head with his hand. He was angry with himself. How he wished he could reach for his brain in his head and toss it out the window. Not only had he found that he *actually* liked Lauralie, their conversations during the ride back from Ernesto's to his hotel had become downright flirtatious.

He sat up on bed and stared out of the window, head swirling with ideas of how to remedy the situation. "It's time to back-peddle," he muttered. Feeling a new sense of determination, he sprang out of bed. *It's best to treat her just like any other client. No strings attached.* Colton had served as a private pilot for many people since he'd left service. However, none was as attractive, or as potentially dangerous as Lauralie.

Colton showered and dressed quickly, eager to leave the upscale hotel Sebastian had booked him in.

Between his blue-collar childhood in Michigan and his time spent overseas, Colton had no stomach for the decadence that his wealthy clients, like the Shaws, enjoyed. He resented extravagance and felt that it was a waste of money when people in their home country and abroad were starving to death. He arrived at the airport with that resentment in his heart.

Colton was doing his usual pre-flight checks when Lauralie entered the jet with loads of shopping bags.

"Looks like you've been doing what you do best." Colton's resentment spilled out in his sarcastic greetings to Lauralie.

Lauralie was stunned by his harsh greeting. She felt like a thousand knives had plunged into her heart. She thought everything — his attitude and thoughts toward her — had changed for the better after their lunch together yesterday. Apparently not! *What's with him today? His tone was harsh.* She glared at him and clenched her jaw. *Idiot!* She closed her eyes and counted to ten to calm her nerves before she lose control and lunged herself toward him and bite his head off.

After counting to ten, her nerves had calmed down. She opened her eyes and a slight smile lined her lips.

"I have something for you... two somethings actually." Lauralie rummaged through one of the bags. She ignored his attitude and pretended everything's normal. But inside, she was boiling.

"Here." She took out two items and thrust

them into his hands.

Colton looked down. There's one expensive-looking maroon-colored velvet box that had a golden word "HERMES" embossed on it. Colton opened the box and in it contained a set of sterling silver Hermes cuff-links.

"I saw those and thought of you," Lauralie said. "The other gift is more sentimental. Have a look." She signaled to the other bag.

Colton removed the plain brown paper from the other package. Inside was a book emblazoned with the logo of the Lana Shaw Foundation. The book contained inspirational artwork, poetry, and stories created by the children at the outreach centers. Colton flipped though the book's pages before flipping his eyes back to Lauralie.

"I can't accept these," Colton said coldly, his face expressionless. He shoved the velvet box that contained the cuff-links back into her hands. "It wouldn't be ethical. It's an expensive gift, and inappropriate, considering our relationship is strictly professional." He held up the book. "This, I will keep... mainly because I know it didn't cost you any money. Now, if you'll please take your seat, we've been cleared for runway."

Colton turned abruptly and retreated into the cockpit, without looking back.

11

Lauralie stood there with her mouth hanging open. She was beyond confused and didn't know what the hell happened to Colton. She opened her mouth to call after him, but nothing came out. The words got stuck in her throat.

Her confusion quickly turned into anger. She felt her anger rising in her, about to explode like a volcano. She clenched her jaw and gritted her teeth. She clutched the velvet box until her hand hurt. She stared at his back so hard as if by doing that, she could burn a hole in his shirt with her gaze. She wanted to burn him alive. She wasn't going to accept his change in attitude without an explanation. She spent the entire flight home fuming mad.

When the jet landed, Lauralie sprang up to her feet from her seat and walked over to the cockpit door. She planted herself firmly outside the door, with her arms folded, waiting for Colton.

"What the hell happened to you?" Lauralie yelled the minute Colton stepped out of the cockpit. She glared at him with fury in her eyes and balled her hands into fists at her sides. Volcano had erupted and lava was spewing out, destroying everything in its path. She looked like a lion ready to pounce on its prey and tear him to pieces.

Colton was startled by what greeted him. He had lingered in the cockpit he thought was long enough to avoid Lauralie and her outbursts, if any. Once he was sure she'd gone, he gathered his things and made his way out slowly. But little did he know that what awaited him would throw him off his feet that he nearly tripped. Enraged Lauralie had been waiting for him, and she was mad as hell. So mad that her whole body shook. He steadied himself against the cockpit door.

"Nothing happened to me," Colton said coolly. He had a pair of shades on which came in handy in a situation like this. It did the job of hiding his expressions perfectly which made reading him impossible. It made Colton seem like he didn't care a hoot about anything and everything that's happening. And this enraged Lauralie even more.

Colton continued, "Nothing has changed, Ms. Shaw. I'm your pilot and you're my client. That's all there is to it. I can't accept the expensive gifts as I'm only a pilot that your father employed." If there's any uneasiness inside, he hid it well. He didn't let it show outwardly.

"But yesterday... I thought..." Lauralie trailed off. Her voice quivered. There's a stinging sensation in her eyes. Tears were slowly welling up which blurred her vision.

"You thought that one lunch would change

my entire opinion of you?" Colton chucked his free hand into his pocket. "You thought, perhaps, that you could give me an expensive, meaningless gift and I'd follow you around like a dog? Those cuff-links only confirm that the press is true about you. You think everyone has a price, right?"

Lauralie's world tumbled down by what he had just said. Her anger quickly turned into hurt. She was more hurt than furious. It's like a million knives pierced through her heart this time. It was so painful that her whole body became numb. She thought she'd found somebody who finally understood her; that Colton's different from anybody else. Apparently, she was wrong.

Lauralie wiped away a tear that had rolled down her cheek with the back of her hand. "The cuff-links reminded me of you, and were intended to be a friendly gesture, not meaningless, or an attempt to buy you in any way." She swallowed a lump behind her throat and continued. "And you're right about the book, I have hundreds of them and that copy probably cost me less than a dollar. But it's incredibly meaningful. It was my idea, my first big project when I took over as the foundation's spokesperson."

They stood there in silence for a moment, staring down at each other before Colton spoke again.

"Let me ask you something, Ms. Shaw. How many of these children have you actually met? How many of them have you comforted? Would you recognize them in public?" He paused. "No, you wouldn't. You approached the entire thing as a savvy business move. You had your lackeys put together this collection, so you could bat your eyes and hock them to your yuppie friends for a hundred bucks a pop. You look like a saint, and everyone else would look like an ass if they didn't buy a copy for charity. Am I close?"

Lauralie shot him a look of pure hatred, at a loss for words. She couldn't believe the false accusations that came out from his mouth.

"Say whatever you want and believe what you want! I don't care!" Lauralie yelled. She couldn't contain her anger anymore.

Lauralie grabbed her bag from the seat and stomped out of the jet. She was determined to have Colton fired before she had to travel again.

AIRLINE PILOTS' COMMITTEE
123 McGill Street
Montreal, Quebec

7 October 2014

Ms. Lauralie Shaw
8700 Santa Monica Blvd
Los Angeles, CA 90000

Dear Ms. Shaw,

Thank you for your letter of 3 October 2014.

I am sorry to hear of the insults being thrown at you by your new pilot, Mr. Colton Dixon. I understand the hurts and distress you've been through. However, we can't put him behind bars as these do not qualify as crimes, as you termed it.

I suggest that you have an amicable talk with your pilot to settle these 'personal issues'.

Why are you interested to know what is my favorite food? Anyway, my favorite food is fried chicken. And I eat it every day.

Yours Sincerely,

Alex T.
Airline Pilots'Committee

12

"I've told you, Lauralie!" Rachel took a sip of the coffee and set the cup back down on the saucer. She propped her elbow on the table and rested her chin on her hand. They've met up at Lauralie's house to discuss about the outreach engagements that Sebastian had asked Rachel to set up.

"Colton had asked for a very specific disclaimer in his contract," Rachel said, drumming her fingers on the table. "Your father had also listed a very specific list of actions that were grounds for termination. As long as he doesn't do anything off of the list, he can't be fired without opening us up to a lawsuit."

Lauralie was upset. It had been two days since she last saw Colton and the mention of his name still made her blood boil to this day.

"That doesn't even sound like a real contract," Lauralie argued, leaning back in the chair. She folded her arms across the chest. "I bet it'd never hold up in court."

"It's a valid contract, Lauralie," Rachel said matter-of-factly, stroking her chin. "Do you think your father's stupid? This was a case of your reputation preceding you, Lauralie. Colton had heard from other pilots how difficult you can be to work with." Rachel took another sip of the coffee.

"Do you think I'm difficult to work with?" Lauralie already knew the answer and was guilty for the most part, but she had to ask nonetheless. It's not that she expected Rachel's reaction to be different, it's just that she didn't want to face the truth. The truth hurt.

Lauralie lowered her gaze to the table. Her eyes seemed to be distant, as if thinking of something.

"Of course not, but the fact is we know each other." Rachel placed her hands on the table and leaned toward Lauralie. "And you don't treat me like the other people who work for you."

Lauralie had known Rachel since high school. She was the closest thing Lauralie had ever had. They had been roommates at school, and she appreciated that Rachel treated her like anyone else, something which she had yearned for.

Unlike those awful girls back east, Rachel hadn't cared one bit who Lauralie's parents were. Even if they were presidents, so what? Rachel was kind, and she's not afraid to point out her faults and mistakes. The girls had lost touch briefly during college, but when the foundation needed a new director, Lauralie had known just who to call.

"So... you do think I'm hard on my employees?" Lauralie asked, eyes still fixed on a spot on the table.

"Lauralie, you have no filter," Rachel explained. "Whatever emotions you're feeling, you take them out on the people around you. Being on the receiving end of that can be overwhelming. And you get really upset when you don't get your way, you have to admit that," Rachel said honestly.

"I don't mean it personally," Lauralie insisted, "most of it, anyway."

"I know that. And they all know that too... mostly. It's just stressful, never knowing what to expect from you."

Lauralie sat quiet for a moment. "So we can't fire him..." Her voice trailed off.

"You're just going to have to get over it. You don't even have to see Colton. Hell, I can tell him to stay in the cockpit when you're onboard."

"Yeah, that would make me look great, wouldn't it? While we're at it, how about I start making the staff wear starched uniforms and forbid them to make eye contact with me?" Lauralie said with biting sarcasm.

"Well, fine then," Rachel said impatiently, "find your own way to deal with him."

"I'm sorry, Rachel. I didn't mean to spill my anger out on you," Lauralie apologized. "He's just so damn frustrating!" She reached for her glass of orange juice and took a long, hard sip.

Rachel noticed Lauralie's unusually weird

behavior. A light bulb lit up in her head, as if she was suddenly enlightened about something. Having known Lauralie for so long, she's beside herself today. Or was it since Colton came into the picture? Rachel broke into giggles shortly after realizing what's going on, if she guessed correctly.

"Stuff like this usually doesn't bother you so much," Rachel teased. "Since when do you care what some asshole thinks about you? Unless you do care what he thinks about you," she said with a naughty, wide grin on her face. "You *do* like him, don't you?"

Cough! Cough! "What?!" Choked by the orange juice, she spat out and spilled some of it onto her dress. She set the glass down on the table. It's a good thing she wore black today and the stain wasn't noticeable. Had she worn white — which was her favorite color — she swore she would strangle Rachel for making such a remark that made this mess out of her. She grabbed a cloth across the table and wiped her dress down.

"Of course I *don't* like him!" Lauralie defended. She felt her face flushing hot. "Have you been listening to me? I hate him! I want him gone! But since we can't make that happen, I guess you're right. Why would I care what he thinks about me?" Contrary to what she said, deep down she meant otherwise.

"I've met Colton briefly when your father

interviewed him. He's gorgeous! He was in the military, wasn't he? Do you think he still has his uniform?" Rachel eyed Lauralie and took another sip of the coffee.

Lauralie thought of the loss Colton had revealed to her. She wouldn't be surprised if he'd gotten rid of anything that reminded him of the Air Force. As much as she wanted to ignore, his painful expression was etched in her mind. She didn't share her thoughts with Rachel. "I couldn't care less if he still has it or not. And I don't care how attractive he is, it doesn't give him the right to be an ass."

"So you think he's sexy?" Rachel wouldn't stop teasing her.

Lauralie rolled her eyes and frowned. "Rachel, can we drop this please? If we can't fire Colton, then I need to call him and let him know about Milan. I'm sure he'll show no judgment at all about flying me across the globe for Fashion Week," she said, sarcasm rearing its head again.

"If he gets judgmental, just put him in his place. He had no problem putting you in yours."

"Yeah, I'll remember that," Lauralie said over her shoulder as she made her way to the phone in the living area. She sat down on her couch, cleared her throat, and dialed Colton's number. He answered on the second ring.

"Hello," Colton greeted in a tone that

suggested to Lauralie he knew who was on the line.

"Hi, this is Lauralie," she said anyway.

"Yeah, I have your number saved in my phone," Colton replied in that impatient tone of his, which infuriated Lauralie. She glanced over at Rachel, who was watching her intently, and made a disgusted face. Rachel gestured with her hands to cool down.

Lauralie turned her attention back to the phone. "Great. Well, I'm calling to let you know that I have a trip scheduled in two weeks. We're going to New York City and then to Milan. We'll be there for eleven days. We leave on the ninth, as early as possible, around six in the morning. We'll spend one night in the city and leave for Milan first thing the next morning," she said in one breath.

"Got it," Colton replied, making mental notes on the dates and the logistic part of the trip. "If you want, we can leave before sunrise," Colton suggested.

"That's fine. You'll have your own room at my hotel, and per diem money for expenses," Lauralie quickly added.

"Great," Colton said again. The silence that followed signaled that he was finished with the conversation.

"Well, I'll see you on the ninth then." And with that, Lauralie hung up the phone without waiting for Colton's response. *This is going to be the worst Fashion Week ever*, she thought to herself.

13

In the days leading up to her trip, Lauralie was filled with anxiety. She thought about what Rachel said. *Maybe she was right? Why did Colton's attitude frustrate me so much unless I really cared what he thought of me?* She shook her head. *That's impossible!* She just couldn't figure out why. She'd met lots of attractive men before and even dated a few of them. But none of them affected her the way Colton did. She couldn't put her finger on what made the pilot so different from the rest.

She went to bed early the night before her flight, but sleep never came. After a restless three hours, Lauralie rose and checked to make sure that she'd packed everything she needed. She glanced at the clock on her bedside table. Four o'clock. It would be another forty-five minutes before Hank arrived to pick her up. She had called Hank last night to inform him that she'd like to set off at four forty-five sharp. She didn't want to get caught in traffic when she arrived in New York City.

Lauralie stepped into the bathroom and turned on the tap. She looked at her reflection in the mirror. The thought of seeing Colton in an hour's time made her anxious. Despite the fact that she missed him, Lauralie didn't want to see him. She didn't know how to react to him later.

Argh! Brushing him aside, she showered quickly, dried her hair and pulled it into a ponytail. She chose a T-shirt and wore a sweatshirt over it and sweatpants, and grabbed a heavy coat to wear after they arrived in New York.

The doorbell rang just as Lauralie finished brewing her coffee. Hank stood in the doorway with a wide grin.

"Good morning, Ms. Shaw," Hank greeted cheerfully as he reached in and took Lauralie's luggage which she had placed by the door earlier.

"Good morning, Hank. I'm sorry that you have to come so early," she apologized as Hank loaded her luggage onto the vehicle.

Lauralie folded her arms and pulled her sweatshirt tighter as she stood in the driveway. The wind was chilly, especially in this wee morning.

"No problem, Ms. Shaw," Hank assured her. "Getting up early keeps me young." He chuckled.

Lauralie considered his words for a while. "But four forty-five is worse than early." She stood in the driveway while Hank continued to load the luggage.

"Hank?" Lauralie called out to him after a long pause. He had finished loading all her luggage onto the limo by then and slammed the door shut. He turned and faced her. "Yes, Ms. Shaw?"

Lauralie thought about the conversation she'd had with Rachel two weeks ago. "I know that I can be difficult sometimes, but I hope you know that I do appreciate you."

"Thank you, Ms. Shaw. You know, I've been around since you were just a baby," Hank reminded her. "I know you're a good person, and I don't take it personally when you get upset," he assured her.

"I'm glad to hear that." Lauralie smiled. *What a relief!*

"Now, let's get you to the airport. Hopefully we'll have an uneventful trip this time round." He winked.

Lauralie slid into the back of the limo and they made their way to the airport.

As they got closer to the airport, loads of butterflies were fluttering in Lauralie's stomach until her stomach ached a little. She didn't know what to expect when she's face-to-face with Colton. Anxiety enveloped her when they pulled up at the hangar an hour later.

Colton sat in the leather seat opposite hers, reading a newspaper. He smiled when she entered the cabin. "Good morning, Ms. Shaw," he greeted her normally. He glanced at his watch briefly. "I take it you didn't hit traffic this morning?"

Lauralie was relieved. Relieved that Colton seemed to want to ignore what had happened between them just as much as she wanted. She relaxed a bit. "It was an uneventful trip," she responded.

"Why are we leaving so early?" Colton asked, raising his eyebrows as if surprised that Lauralie would ever wake up this early in her entire life.

"I'm speaking at an event tonight," Lauralie answered.

Colton paused for a while. "I didn't realize there were any big social events in the city this weekend."

"It's not a social event," Lauralie scoffed and smugly corrected him. "It's a dinner event for children who have lost their mothers to breast cancer."

Colton was surprised. "I'm sorry. I didn't know you do those types of events." This night event would be the first of many more such events Lauralie would do. And her pride didn't allow her to give Colton the impression that this was her first time doing it. She wanted to prove herself. Or rather prove Colton wrong about her.

"It's alright," Lauralie sighed. "There's a lot about me you haven't discovered just yet."

Colton shrugged. "Maybe you're right," he agreed. "We've been cleared for takeoff anytime in the next half-hour. Anna's in the galley fixing some breakfast for you. She should be back any minute."

Colton rose from the chair and marched toward the cockpit. "Enjoy the flight, Ms. Shaw."

Lauralie nodded.

Anna appeared and placed a tray of food in front of her. Colton's voice came over the audio system announcing that they're about to take off in a few minutes. Anna took a seat opposite Lauralie's and clicked her seat belt in place.

"So, how did it go?" Anna spoke in a loud whisper, afraid Colton might overhear the conversation though that's impossible as the heavy-duty door between them was soundproof. "I heard you tried to get him fired. Did he show you any attitude when you got here?"

"No, he was purr-fectly polite." Lauralie took a big spoonful of yogurt which Anna prepared. She then took up a fork and reached for a strip of bacon.

Anna continued, "I also heard about that clause in his contract. What the nerve!"

"It's okay Anna, really," Lauralie assured her. "I just want to forget about it, and I think he feels the same way too." Just then, Anna's stomach growled. Although it's a soft rumbling, it was still loud enough to hear. Anna quickly placed her hands over her stomach in a bid to silence the stomach. She glanced at Lauralie in embarrassment.

"Anna, did you not have breakfast? I know I had you up really early this morning."

Anna blushed. "Hubby and I were up late last night, and I overslept," she explained. "I only got here ten minutes before you."

"Then why didn't you fix yourself something when you were preparing my food?" Lauralie paused and spoke again firmly this time. "As soon as we've reached our altitude and the seat belt sign turned off, you are to go back to the galley and get some food. Feel free to help yourself. What's your favorite soda?" she asked.

"Peach crush." Anna blinked her eyes repeatedly like a little child, wondering why she asked.

"Wonderful. I'll make sure the ground staff puts that on the list of things to keep stocked in the galley." Lauralie grinned.

Anna was surprised by her gesture. Her mouth hanged open and no words came out for a while. "Thank you, Ms. Shaw," she finally managed. "You needn't do that."

"That's another thing." Lauralie pointed at Anna. "I'd like you to stop calling me 'Ms. Shaw, Ms. Shaw'," she said in a mimicking tone. "I'm two years younger than you for god's sake. Just call me Lauralie."

Anna beamed mischievously. Gossips had been flying around. It seemed to confirm what she'd heard were all true. Something seemed to be softening Lauralie, and many believed that it had something to do with her pilot — Colton Dixon. Whatever it was, they were all grateful for the change in Lauralie's attitude, however slight it might be.

Colton's voice came over the speakers again. It was safe to move around the cabin.

"Go, get something to eat," Lauralie insisted. "Could you also help check on Colton before you head to the galley? See if he'd like anything, if you don't mind."

Anna grinned. In all of her years she'd flown with Lauralie, she'd never once asked her to check on the pilot.

14

"Ms. Shaw? Lauralie?" Anna called, patting Lauralie gently on the arms. "We'll be landing at JFK in about half an hour." Anna stood towered over her.

Lauralie stirred and opened her eyes. She stared at Anna and in her trance-like state, wondered for a moment where she was. Then as if suddenly remembering, she smiled. She's going to New York en route to Milan.

"Thank you, Anna." Lauralie yawned, her eyes still half open. She'd been too nervous to sleep the night before. But after her easy encounter with Colton this morning that lifted the weights off her, she was able to nap through most of the flight.

"Ms. Shaw... I'm sorry, I mean Lauralie. Oh gawd, it's going to take some getting used to it." Anna laughed, referring to calling Lauralie by her name. "Anyway, I know you're speaking at the children banquet tonight. I'm just wondering if I could attend?"

"Of course you can, Anna! If you want to attend." Lauralie sat up and stretched. "Though I'm afraid it may bring back sad memories."

"No worries, Lauralie. I'll be alright." Anna shook her head. Like Lana — Lauralie's mom — Anna's mom had died of cancer. Cervix cancer. She was in the last stage when they found out about it —

when all was too late. It definitely threw them off their feet, and plunged the whole family into darkness. Who would have known that a health freak like her, who exercised every other day and watched what she ate, would be plagued with this illness. Life is unfair. It took them a long time, two years in fact, to come to terms with her death.

"I'd love to have a familiar face in the crowd. You know how nerve-wrecking this whole thing is for me." Lauralie laughed nervously. She still couldn't believe that she would be speaking, or rather, encouraging children who had lost a parent, or both, to cancer. Life still had to go on, but this speaking-to-encourage just wasn't her thing.

"That's great!" Anna exclaimed excitedly. She stared into space and paused for a long while, as if thinking of something. "If you don't mind, I'd like to join you when you mingle with the kids after your official speech. Do you think it would be alright if I just sit and talk with some of them?"

"Of course that would be alright, Anna." Lauralie patted her arms lightly. "Do you think it will help?"

"Help them? Or us?" Anna glanced at Lauralie.

"Both!" Lauralie laughed.

"I think it will help us all," Anna nodded and agreed.

Just then Colton's static voice came over the speakers, interrupting them. They were beginning their descent. They returned to their seats and buckled up.

"Do you think Colton would like to come too?" Anna asked as she adjusted and buckled her seat belt. "Do you think he'd find it depressing?"

Lauralie paused and looked at Anna. "We can try asking him. Who knows? It might help him too," she suggested, without revealing the loss that Colton experienced. The loss of his only brother.

Anna thought for a moment. "That's right. He went overseas, didn't he? He probably understands grief better than any of us. My brother is in the Army... or was. He was never the same after his first tour. I can't imagine what they saw over there." She shrugged.

"I can't imagine either." Lauralie swiveled her head from side to side and looked out the window. The jet's wheels were about to meet the runway. They were landing.

"Why don't you invite Colton?" Lauralie suggested. "I feel the gesture may seem more genuine if it comes from you."

Anna thought for a while. "Alright then," she agreed. "Although I think he'd accept the invitation from you too. I think he really likes you," she teased and giggled.

Lauralie felt her cheeks flushing hot. Her heart was beating so hard and fast that she was sure she's going to die of heart attack. She tried to hide her blushing face, but she knew it was too late. The way Anna looked and grinned at her told Lauralie that her emotions were written all over her face. Before she could respond to Anna, the cockpit door opened and Colton appeared. The plane had landed a few moments ago.

Their gaze followed Colton as he walked over to the exit door suavely and swung it open. "After you, ladies." A slight smile lined his lips. As if snapping out of a trance, Lauralie and Anna jumped out from their seats and grabbed their bags, embarrassed. Embarrassed that they'd been staring at his back and his nice butt — way too hard.

The ground crew had already delivered their staircase and was loading their luggage into a long, navy blue limousine. The trio descended the steps, and Colton walked the women to the waiting car.

"You two go on ahead to the hotel," Colton said. "I'd like to do the post flight checks myself and make sure that the jet is in top shape for our long flight tomorrow." He turned and fixed his intense green eyes on Lauralie. Lauralie's heart skipped a beat and almost leapt out from her mouth. That's the power of his gaze on her. Colton continued, "I'll grab a cab when I'm finished."

Breaking the contact between the two, Anna asked, "Colton, would you like to join us at the children banquet tonight? You know... Lauralie will be speaking and we could lend her some support." Lauralie glanced at him, hopeful for a positive response in her heart.

"I didn't bring anything to wear to the banquet..." he began when Lauralie interrupted.

"It's a children banquet, not the Met Gala," Lauralie said. "It's nothing formal. I'm wearing jeans and a sweater. We're serving pizzas, veggie sticks, and ranch dressing."

"Well, I guess that does sound like my kind of party." Colton smiled.

"We could meet in the lobby at six," Lauralie suggested.

Colton nodded. "See you girls at six then." With that, he turned and walked toward the plane.

Lauralie watched his back for a while. *Fashion Week's not going to be so bad after all,* she thought to herself.

15

Lauralie arrived in the lobby fifteen minutes early and paced up and down with anxiety. She was already nervous enough about her speech. And her nervousness was now made worse with Colton attending the banquet as well. *Did I do the correct thing by inviting him?* She began to wonder and feel a brief moment of regret. It was driving her crazy. She was on the verge of chickening out, faking a migraine, and retreating to the safety of her room when Anna appeared at her side.

"Don't worry, Lauralie, you're going to do great," Anna assured her, seeing how nervous she was getting by the minute.

"I'm not so sure about that, I feel like I'm going to be sick."

"Do you get this nervous before all of your events?" Colton's voice startled Lauralie as he approached them from behind. He was dressed in a pale green button-up and tight-fitting, light blue jeans that wrapped up his butt perfectly.

"Would you think less of me if I said yes?" Lauralie laughed nervously, in a bid to cover her anxiety. The more she tried to cover her nervousness, the more it showed.

"Nah," Colton said lightheartedly, shaking his

head. "I think a little bit of stage fright is healthy. It shows you really care about what you're about to do."

"Well, of course I care!"

Colton nodded. "I believe you." His charming eyes were fixed on Lauralie's for a while. Lauralie felt her world exploding in fireworks and blood rushing to her head.

"Shouldn't we be going?" Anna interrupted, breaking the contact — the invisible electric current flowing between the two — yet again. She grinned.

"Ye.. Yes..." Blushing, Lauralie fumbled for words. She turned and walked toward the door. "Rachel has called for the car. It should be here by now."

Without another word, the other two followed her out of the hotel toward a limo that was waiting. A rush of cold wind hit them as they stepped outside. They pulled their sweaters and overcoats tighter around them and hopped onto the car.

The limo carried them far away from the ritzy area their hotel was located in into a much lower income area of the city. Forty-five minutes later, the car stopped in front of their destination — a small storefront with the Foundation's logo painted on its brick exterior.

Colton looked around the surroundings and was surprised by what he saw versus what he expected. "I expected this place to be fancier." He raised his eyebrows.

Lauralie turned and looked at him. "Having a fancy building is not important. What's more important is to be close to the people who need us," Lauralie explained. "We have small centers like this throughout most of the city."

Colton's eyes popped wide open like a goldfish. "You mean you have places like this nationwide?" he asked with a hint of admiration in his voice.

"We have them in most major cities," Lauralie answered. "We don't have as many as we'd like, but we're still growing."

"Lauralie is being modest," Anna interrupted. "She's a fantastic fundraiser. The Foundation has opened thirty new centers since she became the spokesperson."

Colton whistled softly. "That's impressive," he commented. He couldn't help but noticed how Lauralie's peach sweater complimented her skin and hugged her in all of the right places... not to mention how tight her ass looked in her designer jeans. His eyes roamed her body from top to bottom.

Lauralie blushed at the way Colton looked at her. "Thank you," Lauralie mumbled shyly.

"Come on. Let's get inside and get this speech done and over with." Anna glanced over at Lauralie. "In twenty minutes, the scary part will be over and we can all grab some pizza and relax." She grinned.

All three went into the building. Lauralie was brought into a back room behind the stage. The next half hour went by in a blur to Lauralie as the workers at the center were busy prepping the stage and hall, and she, busy pacing up and down a room rehearsing and memorizing her speech.

Laughter and chattering became more apparent as scores of children were assembled in the cafeteria. Lauralie peeped out of the curtain that separated the stage and the back room. She almost fainted. So many children! At least a hundred of them! She broke out in cold sweat.

Now, this is the moment that Lauralie wished never came. Suddenly, all was quiet and hushed in the hall. An emcee came onto stage and gave a brief introduction of the night's programs.

"And now, we'll have Ms. Lauralie!" Applause and whistles broke out as the emcee introduced Lauralie.

You can do this, Lauralie told herself as she took the stage. *You speak in public all of the time. You've told this story over and over again, this is no different.*

But it was different. She'd told the glossed-over version of her mother's battle with cancer to rich people who barely paid attention to her words. People who had never been plagued by this illness before, and not to mention people who didn't understand what cancer was all about. Lauralie could just say whatever she wanted. Nonetheless, all they would do was to just open their checkbook and donate generously.

But these kids were different. They knew the ugly truth about this disease. They wouldn't respond well to anything but the absolute truth. Lauralie had to be careful with what she was about to say. It could make or break them. She awkwardly checked the microphone before she began.

The first few minutes was nerve-wrecking. Lauralie stumbled over her words and stared at her notes the whole time. She struggled to find her words when she realized what she said and her notes were completely out of order. In a moment of panic, she looked out at the audience. A warming calm filled her when she found Colton's gentle gaze. He nodded his head slowly, as if approving and encouraging her to continue.

Putting aside her notes, Lauralie took a deep breath and continued with where she left off. She told her heartfelt, honest version of her story. All this while maintaining eye contact with Colton. It's as if she's telling her story to a friend. She spoke of the sadness and desperation she'd felt during her mother's battle and the soul-crushing heartache of her loss. The longer she spoke, the easier her words came. The children were listening intently, as if hanging on to Lauralie's every word. Toward the end of her speech, not one child was found with dry eyes. Lauralie's story struck a chord in them.

Loud, thunderous applause filled the whole place when Lauralie finished her speech and stepped off the stage. A swamp of kids quickly surrounded her, wanting to hug her. She hugged every one of them, listened to their stories, and answered their questions as best as she could. Just then, a worker came into the hall and announced that the pizza had arrived. The children squealed with delight and ran to sit themselves down at nearby tables.

Lauralie, Colton, and Anna spread themselves out to sit among the children. Lauralie was overwhelmed and felt her emotions rising. She felt that she'd finally done something right. That she'd finally done what her father, Sebastian, would call a worthy cause. Just by telling her story to these children, she'd helped them feel a sense of hope. A hope that told them it's not the end of the world. And that was the main purposes of the foundation, after all.

Time flew past and it was nine o'clock before they knew it. Lauralie was actually disappointed when they had to part ways with the children. She had enjoyed their company as much as they had enjoyed hers. Lauralie, together with Anna and Colton, said their good-byes to the children and made their way back to the limo.

16

"It was a great night!" Lauralie commented once they were in the car and on their way back to the hotel. She was surprised by how much she'd enjoyed the event herself. "I need to tell Rachel to book a less conspicuous car for events like this," Lauralie said as she leaned back and slumped into the seat, tired. She had noticed the way those children were staring at the limo earlier on.

"That's probably a good idea," Anna agreed. "I really enjoyed your speech and everything, Lauralie. Thank you for letting me come along."

"You're welcome to join me anytime you'd like." Lauralie giggled and glanced briefly at Anna. "That goes for you as well," she turned to Colton and said. He'd been silent since they left the center.

"Thank you." Colton gave Lauralie an appraising look. "This evening was certainly enlightening."

"I stumbled during my speech... at the beginning..." Lauralie sighed, sounding disappointed.

"You did fantastic," Anna assured her. "It's a difficult subject to talk about in the first place. The stumbling felt honest and real to the situation."

Lauralie let out a sigh of relief, happy and relieved to have the first outreach event behind her. "I need a drink," Lauralie said once they arrived back at the hotel. "Would you two like to join me at the bar?" She looked from Colton to Anna and back to Colton again as the trio made their way to the elevators.

Anna shook her head. "I told Bob I'd call him as soon as we got back to the hotel. He was worried the evening might bring back painful memories and upset me. But it didn't." She smiled. "It actually made me feel useful."

"I know what you mean," Lauralie agreed "I feel like we may have really helped those kids tonight."

Ding! The elevator sounded and the door opened. "Have a good night, Anna. And send Bob my regards."

"I will." Anna smiled and said her good-bye before disappearing into the elevator.

After Anna was gone, Lauralie turned to Colton. "So what do you say? Are you up for a nightcap?"

"We have a long flight ahead of us tomorrow," Colton responded. "It would be irresponsible for me to drink. But I'd be happy to keep you company."

Her heart fluttered.

They turned and walked into the hotel bar. Lauralie ordered a shot and a beer while Colton settled into a small, cozy booth.

The waiter came with the drinks Lauralie ordered and set them on the table. Colton looked back and forth between the two drinks. "Does it still affect you?" he asked, referring to her mother's death.

A sad smile crossed Lauralie's face. "It was difficult." She lowered her head. "I've put those memories away for so long that I'd forgotten how much they hurt. Until today." She paused long enough to down her shot. "And now, I wonder what my mother would think of me if she knew me now."

"She'd be proud of you, Lauralie. That's what mothers would think. They love their kids unconditionally, and they're proud of everything they do."

Lauralie eyed Colton curiously. "I take it you're close to your mother?" she asked as she signaled a waitress to their table and ordered another shot.

"I'm close to both of my parents. They've always worked hard. They gave us everything they possibly could," Colton explained. Lauralie downed her second shot and ordered a third. "Whoa.. You might want to slow down." He took her hand in his and stopped her.

"I'll be fine. I'm a good drinker," Lauralie assured.

Realizing he had taken Lauralie's hand for a while, Colton released her hand abruptly and cleared his throat. "I think what you did tonight was very brave," he said softly, but clear enough to be heard above the din.

Lauralie blushed. "I really do want to help them. If I'd had someone to talk to and someone who really understood how I felt then, I think a lot of things may have happened differently," she reminisced.

"Yes, you're right." Colton nodded sadly. "If only there were people who understood when I lost —"

"Colton, I'm so sorry —" Lauralie shook her head.

Colton burst out in laughter. "Lauralie, I learn something different about you all the time."

"What are...... you talking..... about?" Lauralie downed another shot.

"Tonight, you've shown me that you're a very sad drunk," Colton teased her playfully.

Lauralie laughed. "I am....... a good...... drinker," she reminded him and patted his arm.

Colton shook his head and laughed. The way Lauralie downed her shots and the way her words slurred like a drunkard showed that she couldn't hold out any longer.

"We have a long flight ahead of us. It's time to go to bed." Colton stood to his feet.

"Go to bed..."

Colton helped Lauralie to her feet and led her through the lobby, into the elevator, and down the hallway to her suite. She fumbled with her keycard for a moment before Colton took it and opened the door for her. He stood by the doorway and waited for her to enter the room. He wanted to make sure she was safe in her own room before retreating back into his room.

Emboldened by the whiskey in her system, Lauralie curled herself around Colton and rested her head on his shoulder.

"Thank you for what you did tonight, during my speech. I wouldn't have gotten through it without you," Lauralie whispered in his ear.

Colton felt his body temperature rising. His body responded to her touch. "You're welcome." His breath was rapid and heavy. Lauralie felt his arousal and pushed her hips into him. Colton looked intently at her porcelain face and ran his fingers through her hair.

Suddenly, he stopped and pulled away abruptly. *I can't do this*, he scolded himself. Lauralie was taken aback by his sudden move.

Without saying a word, Colton swept Lauralie off her feet. She could feel his hard muscles against her body. He lowered her gently onto the bed. "I'm going back to my room. Drink a glass of water before you go to sleep, and be ready to leave by seven in the morning." With that, he turned and walked toward the door. She heard the door closed gently behind him.

Lauralie was confused by what had just happened. She knew Colton desired and wanted her. She thought she was sure of that. Brushing her thoughts aside, Lauralie drank a glass of water as Colton instructed, washed up and changed into her night clothes.

As she climbed into bed, one thing she was sure of was that she wanted Colton Dixon by her side.

17

Lauralie rose early at half-past four the next morning. A brilliant plan had come to her in the middle of the night, and arrangements needed to be made. She called Rachel immediately and explained to her the plan and what needed to be done. After getting off the phone with Rachel, Lauralie showered and took great care in dressing up, fixing her hair and applying make-up to her already flawless face. An hour later, she called Anna and asked her to meet in the lobby for breakfast.

Lauralie arrived at the lobby and found Anna waiting on a couch outside the hotel cafe. She waved to Anna and marched right up to where she was seated. "Good morning, Anna! Sorry and thanks for meeting me this early," she said apologetically and sat down beside her.

Anna smiled. "No problem. It's not really early," she responded and glanced at her watch. "We're due to leave the airport in an hour's time anyway."

They stood up and walked into the cafe. A tall, slender brunette led them to a small table and set menus in front of them. After placing their orders and the waitress gone, Lauralie turned to Anna. "I wanted to talk to you about something," she began. "How would you like to go home?" She beamed.

Anna scratched her head and looked at Lauralie, confused. "Home? Am I fired?"

"No, no!" Lauralie waved her hands frantically. "I was just... You know... You've just gotten married," she explained. "You're a newlywed. Eleven days away from your new husband is a long time. This is the longest trip I have ever scheduled, and I feel bad for keeping you away from Bob."

This was unlike Lauralie. Since little, she would always have someone serve her. Her parents would make sure of that and it had become part of her life. When she's grown and began to travel frequently, she would always have someone serve her during flights. Especially long ones. What Lauralie just said was very unusual of her. Anna felt something's fishy going on and decided to probe further. "But... don't you need me?" Anna eyed Lauralie suspiciously.

Lauralie looked down at her own fingernails and avoided eye contact with Anna. Just then, the waitress appeared with their muffins and coffee. She set their orders before them.

Lauralie could have jumped up, hugged and kissed the waitress for appearing at the right time. This embarrassing and tense time. Lauralie looked up at the waitress and mumbled her thanks before looking down at her fingernails again. The waitress smiled and disappeared into the kitchen.

"I'm tired and I think I'll probably sleep through the entire flight," she finally managed after a long silence. "Anyway, I can fetch my own snacks. So you don't have to worry about that." She was twirling her fingers.

Anna observed her. She was not telling the truth. Having known Lauralie for so long, she knew her every movement. Anna reached for the muffin and took a bite. "I feel like you're not telling me something." She hesitated before continuing. "Did I upset you in any way?" She took a sip of the coffee, eyes fixed on Lauralie.

Lauralie continued twirling her fingers. The weird expression on Anna's face told her that the only way she was going to convince Anna that nothing was wrong was by telling her the truth. The whole truth, even if it's embarrassing.

Lauralie took a deep breath. Reached for the muffin and took a huge bite off it before she began relating to Anna what happened in the doorway of her hotel room last night. As Lauralie talked, Anna's eyes grew wider and wider as if it's going to pop out of her head. A wide grin spread across her face. The more she talked, the more excited Anna was for her.

By the time Lauralie finished, Anna was giggling and laughing excitedly. "So, you want me out of the way, so you can work your charm on him?" Anna teased.

Lauralie blushed. She wished the earth would open up and swallow her. This was just too embarrassing to admit. Especially for Lauralie. "I guess... yeah."

"I have one condition." Anna raised her index finger.

"I'll still pay you for the entire eleven days..." Lauralie began, thinking that was what Anna referred to.

Anna swiveled her head from side to side and waved both her hands. "Don't be ridiculous. That's not part of the deal." She laughed. "The condition I have for you is..." She looked at Lauralie mischievously. "Is that you have to call or text me with updates every night. Don't make me go wondering what the two of you are up to for the next ten days."

Lauralie pointed at Anna and blinked. "You got it." She giggled like a little girl.

Anna beamed triumphantly. She'd gotten the truth out of Lauralie. In fact, she felt relieved that she wasn't the problem. "I knew you're both meant for each other," Anna chirped excitedly as they finished their muffins and coffee. "I knew it the moment Colton stepped on board the jet. I hope you two get together." Anna held and squeezed both Lauralie's hands across the table.

"Let's not get ahead of ourselves." Lauralie

squeezed Anna's hands in return. "I think you were right. He doesn't want to want me. This doesn't mean he doesn't want me. There's a difference," Lauralie said thoughtfully. "I need some time alone with him to figure out why and see if I can fix it."

"I have a good feeling about this, Lauralie." Anna grinned and glanced at her watch. "It's time to get going."

Lauralie smiled and wished that she felt the same too.

18

Lauralie returned to her room and dialed Colton's number. There was no answer after countless rings. She hung up in disappointment. Just then, her hotel phone rang, startling her.

"Hello?" Lauralie rushed to pick up the phone, expecting to hear Colton's voice.

"Ms. Shaw?" the voice on the other side replied. It's not Colton. "This is Mr. Jones at the front desk. Mr. Dixon left a message for you. He'd like you to know that he's left for the airport. He said he would meet you there."

A wave of disappointment hit her. It was as if her heart sank to the bottom of the bottomless sea. "Alright, thank you very much," she responded. "Would you please call for my car? I'll be leaving in twenty minutes."

"Of course, Ms. Shaw. I'll make the arrangements immediately."

"Thank you." Lauralie clicked off the phone.

A thousand thoughts ran through her mind. *So, Colton was keeping his distance from me yet again*, she thought. *Well, let's see how much distance he could manage while we were on the jet for sixteen hours all alone.* She smirked to herself.

Anna and Lauralie rode in nervous silence to the airport. Lauralie instructed the driver to drop

Anna off at the commercial terminal before dropping her where her jet was.

When they arrived, Lauralie stepped out of the car. Colton was doing his usual pre-flight checks. Their eyes met and they held for a while. She then flicked her eyes to his left. He was not alone. Standing beside him was a stunning, tall, curvy redhead girl. A tightness strangled her heart. She couldn't breathe properly, let alone think properly.

Lauralie staggered up to them. She couldn't walk properly too — her legs had turned jelly.

"Good morning, Ms. Shaw," Colton greeted, with that usual emotionless, formal tone of his. "Where's Anna?" Colton craned his neck to look behind Lauralie, as if expecting to see Anna there.

"I sent her home," Lauralie managed. Flicking her eyes to the redhead girl, she greeted. "Hello." Her breath caught in her throat, making it difficult for the words to come out. Suddenly consumed by anger, she demanded. "I'm Lauralie Shaw. May I ask who are you, and what are you doing here?" She made sure to make known to her who she was — the great Lauralie Shaw whom everyone adored.

Taken aback by the harsh greeting, the redhead girl opened her mouth and was about to speak when Colton interrupted. "This is Gloria Capshaw. She's my co-pilot on our flight to Milan."

"Co-pilot?" Lauralie responded in annoyance.

Colton hadn't mentioned anything about this co-pilot thing to her at all. Her eyes searched Colton's face hungrily, demanding more answers. It was as if by searching his face, answers would just pop out.

"This is the first time I've heard of any co-pilot thing," Lauralie said angrily, shooting Colton a dagger stare.

"With fuel stops, the flight to Milan would be seventeen hours. It's against regulations for a pilot to fly that many hours alone," Colton explained patiently. "And I'll have to stretch, use the bathroom and eat. Surely you don't expect me to stay behind the controls for seventeen hours straight?" He took out his pair of stupid shades and put them on.

Suddenly feeling stupid, Lauralie flinched. She felt bad for the harshness she'd shown earlier. She inner-kicked herself for kicking a big fuss. "Of... of course not..." Lauralie stammered. She turned to Gloria. "Welcome on board, Ms. Capshaw," she said. "If you'll excuse me, I would like to get some rest." Lauralie yawned. She then turned to Colton and instructed. "I don't want to be disturbed. I'd like to get full rest."

Colton nodded. "Of course, Ms. Shaw." He couldn't contain the burning question any longer — his curiosity about Anna. He hesitated before asking. "What happened to Anna? Was she dismissed?" He adjusted and pushed up his pair of shades on the bridge of his nose. A slight smile lined his lips and a soft snort escaped from his throat.

This infuriated Lauralie. She glared at Colton. The careless way he asked her about Anna angered her even more. It was as if her hobby was to fire people.

"She's not dismissed," Lauralie growled. "I sent her home to be with her husband. Eleven days is a long time, and I thought she might need the support after all of last night's emotions." She turned and began walking up the jet. "As I said just now, I'm going to bed. I'll see you in Milan, Mr. Dixon." With that, Lauralie stomped onto the jet.

Lauralie collapsed into her bed, thinking of what just happened. Her plan doesn't seem to be working out at all. After ten minutes of tossing and turning in bed, she fell asleep. As instructed, none of the pilots came to disturb her.

About midway through the flight, Lauralie was woken up by Colton's static voice over the speakers. They were descending to refuel. Lauralie was too tired that she fell back asleep again while the pilots exited and re-entered through the cabin. After refueling, they were on their way again.

A jerk woke Lauralie up. She sat up and looked out the window. They'd arrived in Milan. The jet's wheels had just met the runway and was getting ready to stop. The minute it stopped and the staircase attached to the door, Lauralie grabbed her bags and exited the jet hurriedly before both pilots could emerge from the cockpit.

With the time difference, it was already the next afternoon in Milan. Lauralie felt so refreshed after having a full, undisturbed sleep on the plane. She hardly felt any jet-lag at all.

Lauralie was still mad. Very mad and she had long given up on the plan she'd had.

Lauralie took a long shower after checking into her suite. She looked over the itinerary Rachel had typed up for her. That evening, she was set to meet with a large group of models who had agreed to shoot as cover models for the Foundation's calendar. Fashion Week would officially begin the next day, and every moment of her time would be spent kissing up the asses of potential donors.

Lauralie glanced at the the clock on the side table. To her astonishment, it was already five-thirty! How time flies. She unpacked her luggage and flipped through the stack of gorgeous clothes she'd brought with her. She selected a slinky, teal, silk mini-dress to wear for the evening. Lauralie let her long, honey-blonde hair lay straight down her back, and spent almost two hours fixing her hair and make-up.

Whenever there were big events like these, there would be paparazzi and reporters chasing after celebrities and the who's who. One thing's for sure, they would be stalking her and everyone else for the rest of the week. So Lauralie made sure she wouldn't leave her hotel room without makeup and full dress-up.

At a quarter to eight, Lauralie glanced at her own reflection in the full-length mirror one last time. She looked stunningly gorgeous. She smiled and gave herself a nod of approval. She closed the door gently behind her and made her way down to the lobby.

Heads turned when Lauralie stepped out of the lift lobby. The group of models were already waiting for her at the hotel salad bar, where they would be having salad buffet before hitting town.

In twenty minutes, everyone was seated and enjoying their salads. Lauralie showed them the layouts they were considering for the calendar. They discussed about possible shooting locations and everyone agreed to the terms of the photo-shoot.

When they're done eating their full, the models whose shows weren't until later in the week offered to take Lauralie to a famous pub in town which was frequented by top celebrities and models. They spent the night drinking and dancing away with some of the world's most beautiful people. As expected, they'd had to stop several times for obligatory paparazzi shots.

Before Lauralie knew it, it was two o'clock past midnight and it was time to go back to the hotel.

James, one of the male models, offered to escort her back to the hotel as he was on his way to meet his boyfriend for a nightcap. He helped Lauralie to her feet as she was a bit drunk and bundled her into a waiting car.

    When they reached the hotel, James supported and held on to Lauralie's waist as they walked through the hotel lobby and entered the elevator. When they stepped out of the lift, Lauralie lifted her eyes to the direction of her room and gasped loudly. There, waiting outside of her room, half-way down the hall, was Colton Dixon.

19

Colton's eyes bore through Lauralie's as if he was ripping through every of her tendons and muscles. Sensing something's not right, James released Lauralie abruptly.

Where have you been? An unspoken question shot through the air to Lauralie. Telepathy.

As if Lauralie understood, she glared at Colton. *None of your business!*

Who is he? Colton swept his eyes swiftly to James and back to Lauralie.

None of your business. Lauralie rolled her eyes.

They stared down at each other for a while. James swiveled his head from Lauralie, to Colton, then back to Lauralie again. He stood there, motionless and helpless.

As if suddenly cutting off the invisible telepathy current, Lauralie turned to James. "Thank you for seeing me back safely. Please tell Fernando that I'm sorry to have kept you," she said apologetically.

"Are you going to be okay?" James eyed Colton suspiciously. "I can stay for a while, if you'd like," he offered.

Lauralie shook her head. "I'll be fine," Lauralie responded. "Mr. Dixon is my pilot. He's harmless," she assured James.

"Alright, I'll see you tomorrow then? The Charles Fontaine show?" James reached out for the button of the elevator.

"I wouldn't miss it." She gave a weak smile.

James said his goodbye and disappeared into the elevator.

Lauralie turned to Colton. He was standing right in front of her room, and she needed to get past him in order to get into her room. After partying so hard at this wee hour, she was dead tired. All she wanted right now was to plop down onto the big, comfy bed which was calling out to her. She had no choice but to brace herself and walked toward Colton to get into her room.

Lauralie stopped in front of Colton, expecting him to make way. But he refused to move.

"Let me guess, you just woke up?" Lauralie asked sarcastically. "Jet-lag can be a real bitch. Fortunately for me, I was well rested throughout the flight. But unfortunately for you, I'm exhausted now, and in no mood to keep you company while you adjust to the time difference." She shot a look at him. "If you'll excuse me, I'm going into my room."

Colton stood his ground, refusing to move.

Lauralie shoved him hard. He jerked aside. She took out her keycard and slid it down the keycard lock to open the door. The red light lit up, signaling that opening the door wasn't successful. She tried again and the same thing happened.

"You seem to have problems with this." Colton took the keycard from her and opened the door.

Lauralie shoved past him to enter the room. "Anyway, what are you doing here, Mr. Dixon?" Lauralie demanded, standing at the door and refusing to let him into her room. They stood in the doorway, staring down at each other, for what seemed to be eternity.

Colton finally broke the heavy silence between them. "I called your room and nobody answered. I wanted to see if you'd like to have dinner with me. I figured you'd gone out. But then I called back at ten o'clock and you still weren't in... and then at one a.m... I was concerned."

She smirked. "You needn't be concerned about me, MR. Dixon." She put an emphasis on the word 'Mr'. "I've been taking care of myself for a long time. I don't need to be chaperoned."

"I just wanted to make sure you made it back okay." Colton lowered his eyes to the floor. "I'll leave you alone now." He turned and walked toward the elevator.

Lauralie watched his back as he walked away. Although she was very upset now, half of her wanted him to stay. Very badly.

"Why the hell do you care?" she shouted after

him.

Colton stopped midway in his tracks with his back facing her. He shook his head. "Honestly, I don't know." He turned to face her. "You're a selfish, spoiled child, Lauralie... most of the time. But every now and then, you surprise me. You intrigue me. I guess I'm trying to figure out which one is the real you... the girl who spends thousands of dollars on one pair of shoes? Or the down-to-earth girl who eats with the locals and volunteers with children?"

"Well, maybe I'm both," Lauralie shot back. "Maybe I'm a shoe whore who loves helping sad kids. Have you ever thought of that?"

"I have... I've thought about so many things since our lunch together in Aspen. I think you have too, right?"

"What does it matter?" Lauralie snapped. "I'm under the impression that, like me or not, you have no desire to actually be with me. Am I correct?"

"Let me explain —" he began.

"I don't need an explanation, Mr. Dixon. I need to go to bed and get some sleep now. You're not denying that I'm right, so why don't you just go find something to do? My schedule is booked through the entire week. I'll see you at the airport on the twentieth."

With that, Lauralie stormed into the room and slammed the door shut.

20

Since their showdown at the hotel that night, Lauralie refused to acknowledge Colton's existence for the rest of her stay in Milan. Her days were filled with business lunches, and her evenings spent at the shows of designers who donated to the Foundation.

By the end of the trip, Lauralie had not only secured the models for the calendar, but also raised enough money to open yet another outreach center. True to her word, she would update Anna — her flight attendant and now friend - every night. Anna had advised Lauralie to put aside her pride and reconcile with Colton, but she refused to listen. "Screw him, and whatever problems he has." This was Lauralie's reply to Anna every time she brought up the reconciliation.

The hectic week was finally over. Lauralie arrived at her jet on the morning of her long flight back to New York City. She found Gloria busy doing some pre-flight checks on the ground. They nodded and exchanged greetings briefly with each other. Turning aside, she noticed a silver-haired man standing together with Colton at the foot of the ladder leading up to the jet.

"Ms. Shaw," the silver-haired man greeted warmly, extending his hand to her. "I'm Frank Cotton. I'll be your co-pilot on your trip back to the

States." He smiled.

Lauralie took his hands. "It's a pleasure to meet you, Mr. Cotton," Lauralie greeted. "I don't know if Mr. Dixon informed you, but we don't have an attendant flying together with us today." She looked briefly at Colton. All that had happened between them seemed to dissipate into thin air. Or rather, she pretended nothing had ever happened. She wanted nothing to do with him. "If you'd like anything to eat or drink, please let me know over the speaker and I'll be happy to bring you whatever you'd like."

Frank and Colton stood rooted to the ground and stared at her with wide eyes, as if surprised by her out-of-the-ordinary gesture. Frank finally managed, "Well, that's much appreciated, Ms. Shaw. I can't say I've ever flown for a nicer client." He grinned. "If you'll excuse me, I'll check with the tower and see when we're cleared for a runway." With that, Frank disappeared up onto the jet.

"After you." Colton turned to Lauralie and gestured to the staircase. She filed past him and he followed closely behind her up the staircase. Colton leaned down to her ear. "That was a little much, don't you think? Are you trying to sweet-talk your way into convincing ol' Frank to work for you, once you've managed to get me fired?" he smirked.

Lauralie stopped mid-way up the staircase and

turned abruptly to face Colton. It startled him that he almost tumbled down the stairs. They were standing so close. Just a breath away. "Like you said our first day, Mr. Dixon, you're the pilot. Your job is to take me where I want to go, when I want to go. Right now, I want to go home. And I want to go home now. If that would be all, I'm going to get myself something to drink before we take off. Would you like anything?" She stared into his eyes.

Colton composed himself and stated curtly, "No thank you." For some reason, he found that he really liked sparring with Lauralie. And without him realizing it, the fact that she kept calling him 'Mr. Dixon' with that nonchalant tone of hers hurt him. Deeply.

***

Five hours into the flight, Colton had his chance to escape the cockpit. They were flying on autopilot over the ocean, and Frank offered to watch the controls for awhile and let Colton take a break.

Lauralie was reading some magazines in her soft leather chair when Colton entered the cabin. He marched to a seat across from her and sat down, eyes never leaving her all this while.

"That night —" Colton began.

Lauralie looked up from what she was reading and interrupted. "For heaven's sake Mr. Dixon, can't we just put it to rest? I intrigue you. But you don't want to be with me. We have nothing to talk to each other about."

"Lauralie, would you just let me talk?" Colton's eyes bore into hers. "You cut me off that night at the hotel. You slammed the door in my face. But there's no escaping this conversation now. I have something I want to say and you're going to listen." He pursed his lips and narrowed his eyes.

Colton's gaze sent shivers down Lauralie's spine. She was startled by the fierceness of his tone. "Fine," she said after a few moments of silence. "Say what you want to say." Lauralie's gaze shifted back to the magazine and she flipped it so hard as if she was going to tear it apart. As if she was going to tear Colton apart.

"You accused me that night of wanting you and not wanting you. And you're absolutely right. When you act like the girl I saw at the diner, the girl who spoke to those children, I want nothing more than to be with you." His gaze softened. "That night in the hotel, it was all I could do to not follow you into your hotel room. Pulling away took all of the strength I had. Believe me."

Lauralie looked up at him. "But you pulled away," Lauralie responded. "Why?" Her eyes filled with hurt.

"So many reasons Lauralie." Colton looked away. "For one, I work for you and your father. It wouldn't be right for me to start a personal relationship with you."

Lauralie shook her head. "I think my father would be thrilled if we're together. He'd probably think you'd settle me down." Since she'd met Colton, her attitude had changed — for the better. Her staff and the people around her had noticed this as well.

Colton regarded her for a moment. "That may be so." He paused before continuing. "But you're still my boss. If we start seeing each other and if things end badly, it could make for some uncomfortable traveling experiences down the road."

"I disagree," Lauralie countered. "If things end badly, we wouldn't even have to see each other. I think we had both proven that we're good at avoiding each other, even if we're stuck on a jet for a day straight."

Colton nodded. "Okay. I'll concede the first two points," Colton finally agreed. "But there are other reasons us getting together is a bad idea, Lauralie." He sighed. "I'm not like you, I'm not built for your kind of lifestyle. The kind, sweet side of you is irresistible. But when I think of being hauled along to one of those god-forsaken fashion shows, or having my picture on the cover of the gossip rags, I feel like I'm going to be sick," he explained patiently.

"As you are an alpha-male, I'd never expect you to tag along to the fashion shows. I won't deny that I love them. I love the clothes, I love the excitement, but I'm perfectly happy attending them alone. As far as the photos go, do you think I enjoy that?" Lauralie's eyes brimmed with tears. "Do you think I love having my pictures taken while I'm pumping gas or leaving the gym? How do you think I felt about it when I was little? I couldn't even go to preschool because the paparazzi staked out the building." She reached out for a napkin seated on a small table between them.

"Still, Lauralie," Colton looked at Lauralie with those mesmerizing eyes that any girl would swoon over. "I know myself. As much as I'm attracted to you, I know that the stress would get to me, and it would destroy us."

"Then I don't know why we had to have this conversation, unless you're trying to convince me that you're right because you can't convince yourself," Lauralie barked. "That's not going to happen. I want you," she blurted out before she could stop it. "There, I said it. I think you're sexy, and genuine, and honorable. You make me want to be a better person. But if you're too weak to be with me, so be it."

Before Lauralie could continue, Colton rose from his seat, marched over to her, lean in and tilt her chin up. Then, what happened next made Lauralie turned jelly. He gave her the most forceful, passionate kiss that anyone could ever have. At least to her.

After what seemed to be an eternity Lauralie hoped would not end, Colton pulled away. "Did that feel weak to you?" His voice was hoarse.

"N.... No," Lauralie muttered, in a state of shock. "There... there was nothing weak about that." She gazed into his eyes.

As if suddenly remembering he was on the clock, Colton planted a kiss on Lauralie's lips again. This time, gently. "I need to get back to Frank. I'll see you soon when we land." He winked and pulled away from her reluctantly. They gazed at each other for a while more before Colton disappeared into the cockpit.

21

Lauralie spent the rest of the flight eager with anticipation. Fire crackers went off inside her and her heart was beating so fast that she felt like she was going to explode. She giggled to herself like a schoolgirl falling in love. She was so excited! As what had been promised, Lauralie grabbed her phone in her bag and sent a long message to Anna, detailing what just happened.

Lauralie's phone beeped. *Really that happened?* came Anna's reply.

Yup!! :) Lauralie replied and grinned to herself.

Lauralie's phone beeped again. *OMG! Congratulations! Happy for ya! :)* Anna replied.

I'm over the moon right now! Can't wait to see where this brings us! Lauralie replied.

You should be! Good for ya! Wish you all the best! Anna replied.

:) Lauralie replied with a smiley emoticon.

Lauralie smiled to herself. She chucked her phone aside and glanced at her watch. Still four more hours to go before they land. She can't wait to land. She closed her eyes, willing herself to sleep. But sleep never came. She was too excited to sleep. The image of Colton kissing her kept floating in her mind.

***

Someone tapped Lauralie's shoulders lightly. She opened her eyes to find Colton towering over her, with a wide smile on his face. Lauralie had drifted off to sleep.

"We'll be arriving at JFK in twenty minutes," Colton whispered in her ears, fingers tracing along her jawline gently.

Lauralie smiled and stretched with a yawn. "Thank you," she mouthed the words and planted a kiss on his lips. He returned the kiss.

"There will be a car waiting," Lauralie said. "You could ride with me," she suggested, to which Colton nodded.

Lauralie grinned.

"See you later." Colton winked.

Lauralie admired his tall and strong-built back as Colton returned to the cockpit. Her eyes wandered down to his small and firm ass.

Twenty minutes later, they landed. Colton and Frank emerged from the cockpit a few moments later. Unlike the last few trips, Lauralie was there to meet them this time.

"It's lovely to fly with you, Ms. Shaw. I gave Colton my contact information. If you're ever in need of a co-pilot, I hope you'll give me a call," Frank said.

Lauralie nodded. "Of course, Mr. Cotton.

Until next time." Lauralie smiled. Frank grabbed his bag and marched down the staircase into the terminal.

Turning to Colton, she said, "The car should be outside, we'll meet there after customs clearance."

Colton was already at the car when Lauralie stumbled out of the terminal forty-five minutes later, with hands full of big and small shopping bags. Unlike Colton who had nothing to declare, Lauralie had purchased a large assortment of clothing and souvenirs in Milan. That explained why it took her so long to emerge from the terminal.

Colton rushed to take the bags from her and loaded them onto the waiting car. He held open the door for her.

Lauralie smiled and mumbled her thanks.

"Good evening, Ms. Shaw," the driver greeted her with a wide grin as they slid into the car. "To The Plaza?" The driver glanced at Lauralie in the rear mirror.

"Yes please," Lauralie responded and shot a devious look at Colton. "As fast as possible."

22

Four blissful days passed, with Lauralie and Colton falling deeper and deeper in love each day. They had extended their stay in New York for another five days on their own accord. They wanted to enjoy each other and have some lone time together, just like every other normal couple.

To their great relief, the press hadn't caught wind of their spontaneous vacation. The rumor mill churned with explanations as to why Lauralie hadn't been seen in public since leaving Fashion Week. One story claimed that she'd had a bad reaction to Italian ecstasy and was receiving medical treatment at an undisclosed European hospital. Another story had her fleeing to Dubai with a scandalous Arabian prince. These, and other rumors, became the running jokes between Colton and Lauralie while they enjoyed their getaway.

On the fifth morning in New York, Lauralie's cell rang. She stirred and looked at Colton who was laying beside her. He was still sound asleep, oblivious to the ringing of her cell. She smiled at the sight of him. She grabbed her cell from the night table beside her and glanced at it. Rachel.

"Hi Rachel," Lauralie answered lazily.

Rachel was about to say something when the hotel phone rang, which startled Colton. He scowled.

Lauralie glanced at Colton and giggled at his comical reaction. Hotel phones were always so loud and screeching.

"Rachel, hold on a second," Lauralie said as she walked to the phone on the opposite side of the room. "The hotel phone is ringing."

Without giving a chance for Rachel to speak, Lauralie picked up the phone. "Hello?" she answered, stifling a yawn as she cradled the receiver on her shoulder.

"Hello, Ms. Shaw. This is Brian from the front desk. I just wanted to let you know that there are several reporters outside of the hotel." He paused before continuing. "They aren't allowed in the lobby, but we can't make them leave the sidewalk. We, here at The Plaza, understand that our guests appreciate their privacy. If you'd like to leave the hotel without being photographed or followed, your driver could utilize our underground parking lot if you'd like."

Lauralie froze and turned pale. She glanced at Colton nervously. Dread filled her heart. "Y.. Yes Brian, thank you. We will certainly take advantage of that."

Lauralie held on to the hotel phone even after Brian hung up, frozen in place. Sensing something was wrong, Colton asked, "What happened?"

Lauralie shifted her gaze to Colton. Her mouth hang open as if trying to talk, but no words came out. As if suddenly remembering Rachel was on the line, Lauralie took up her cell. Just then, Colton's cell rang and he answered.

"Ra... Rachel?" Lauralie called out nervously. She listened intently as Rachel talked for the next ten minutes. She stole glances at Colton. His face had turned grim and color drained from his face. Lauralie was fearful. Will this be the end of their relationship? She knew too well that Colton hated all these from the get-go.

"Well... that depends on what you consider bad," Rachel continued. "I've sent you pictures while you were on your hotel phone. I'd do damage control, but there's really been no damage done." Rachel paused before continuing. "If anything, I think these could help your reputation, not hurt it."

"I'm not so sure about that," Lauralie muttered apprehensively as she watched Colton's entire body tensed up. "I'll take a look at the pictures you sent and call you back."

Lauralie hung up and scrolled her phone nervously.

Hollywood Sweetheart Slumming It In The City was scrawled across the top of a collection of pictures of her and Colton in New York. One picture showed them entering The Plaza on their first night in the city. In another, they were stretched across a blanket in Central Park. And while each picture showed them in a different setting, their intimate moments were captured in them all.

Lauralie's eyes grew wider as she scrolled through the images. She felt sick to her stomach.

"Well," Colton interrupted, startling Lauralie that she dropped her cell. She didn't know when he had ended his call.

"I am so sorry." Lauralie's eyes welled up with tears. "I don't know how they found me...." Lauralie sobbed, unable to continue.

Colton sat in silence. He was upset. But he knew Lauralie was more upset than him.

Colton softened. "I knew all these were inevitable," he began. "If we're going to be together, the press was bound to figure it out. Honestly, I don't like it. I think we would have to move a little more stealthily in the future." He ran his fingers through his already tousled hair.

Lauralie knew Colton had every right to be offended. "You're the best man I've ever known. This is the farthest from 'slumming it' I have ever been. Let Rachel release a statement. Things will only get worse if we ignore this. We can acknowledge our relationship, provide a little background information on yourself, and then respectfully ask for our privacy. If this is okay for you?" She looked at him with pleading eyes.

"You think that's the best way to handle

this?" Colton wasn't sure this was the way to do it. He didn't like the idea of his privacy being invaded.

Lauralie nodded. "I think it's our only choice." She paused. "Those pictures are out there, and there's no taking them back. We don't want to look like we're hiding something... My mom and dad used to allow paparazzi to take two pictures each in exchange for leaving them alone."

"I'm not sure if I'm ready for that." Colton stood up and walked over to Lauralie. "But I guess you're right about asking Rachel to release a statement."

Lauralie heaved a sigh of relief. "Rachel already has one prepared. I'll tell her to release it. And the hotel has made arrangements for us to leave from the underground parking area."

"At least they waited for our last morning here." They had planned on leaving for Los Angeles this morning. Colton gave a weak smile and pulled Lauralie into his embrace. He kissed her gently on her forehead.

Lauralie looked up at him. "You sure you can handle this?" She wanted to be sure.

"If it means I get to be with you, I can handle anything," Colton assured her.

Lauralie gave a weak smile. Things didn't turn ugly between them like what she'd expected after all.

23

Lauralie called Rachel the moment they touched down in Los Angeles. "Does the press know where we are?" Lauralie asked anxiously.

"I don't think so," Rachel replied. "The paparazzi's still staked out in the city. By the way," she thought for a moment, "there's also a large group set up at LAX hoping to catch you on your way home. I've arranged for two discrete Hondas with drivers in plain clothes to pick you guys up at the hangar. Hank is also there with the limo. He'll divert the paparazzi's attention while you guys get onto the Hondas separately. He's good at it."

"Got it, Rachel. Thank you so much." Lauralie was grateful to have Rachel as her assistant. She always had everything planned out nicely with Lauralie's well-being in mind. Lauralie relayed to Colton what Rachel had told her.

Colton nodded and smiled. He was glad that Rachel had made such arrangements.

"We'll come up with a game-plan tomorrow." Lauralie grinned.

Colton pulled her close and kissed her lightly on her lips. "Thank you for the fantastic vacation." He gazed longingly into her eyes.

Lauralie returned his kiss. They grabbed their

bags and disembarked the jet separately, within twenty minutes of each other. Both kept a reasonable distance between them as they cleared the customs and walked to the two waiting Hondas.

Once Lauralie settled into the car and got past the paparazzi undetected, she heaved a sigh of relief. Just as she was wondering how Colton was getting along, her phone beeped.

Successful evasion! I miss you already :) It was Colton.

I miss you too.. Lauralie replied and broke out into a broad smile.

24

"Lauralie, I'm so happy for you!" Anna exclaimed.

Anna and Rachel sat in Lauralie's bedroom, listening to Lauralie as she told them of her escapades with Colton. Lauralie had invited both, her closest confidante, to her house for high-tea.

"But just think, Lauralie, if you had listened to me, your romance could have started in Milan," Anna plopped herself down onto Lauralie's bed.

Lauralie shook her head. "I'm not sure about that, Anna." Lauralie glanced at Anna briefly. "I think long flights helped to cool things down. You both know how I get when I lose my temper, I needed that time to cool down."

"I wish I could have seen your face when you met that woman pilot. What's her name? Gloria?" Rachel giggled.

Lauralie nodded.

Anna burst out laughing, imagining Lauralie's comical reaction. "I bet you were furious and jealous. I almost wish I would have stayed with you!"

"I did get jealous." Lauralie blushed. "I'm sure it was written all over my face. Gloria must be thinking I'm some kind of nut," she groaned in embarrassment.

"Who cares what Gloria thinks?" Rachel

shrugged. "The most important thing to do right now is to stop the paparazzi from spreading worse rumors."

"We need to come up with a plan." Lauralie looked at both girls. "Colton understood and has accepted that he'll have to deal with it. But I really don't know how much he can take." She shrugged. "I can take everything as I've been there, done that. It happens all the time. But as for Colton, uh-uh." She shook her head. As a non-public figure, Colton had never been exposed to the media. It would be a great shock to him especially with all the attention he's getting and bad press.

"That 'slumming it' article was pretty harsh," Anna said.

"I've been doing a lot of thinking about this," Rachel began. "What if we start planting false leads? I could call and make reservations at one restaurant, and you could enjoy a stress free meal somewhere else?" She paused for a while. "We'll also have to figure out something with the cars... the limo is conspicuous... so is your Aston Martin... and I'm sure by now the paparazzi knows what Colton is driving already."

"I like the false leads idea." Lauralie nodded slowly. "But I don't see a way around the cars." She glanced curiously at Rachel. "What are we supposed to do? Get a new rental car every few days?"

"That's not a bad idea," Anna agreed and sprang up from the bed.

"That could get expensive," Lauralie scowled and shook her head.

Rachel and Anna laughed, as if that was the greatest joke they had heard all week. Fancy Lauralie to say it was expensive when she had all the money in the world!

"How much do you spend buying clothes and eating out in a week?" Rachel sneered. "You can rent a Ford or Honda for about hundred bucks a week."

"Okay, you have a point," Lauralie conceded. "Could you call tomorrow and arrange for short-term rentals?"

Rachel nodded. "Sure, I'll get Wanda to do it. It's much safer that way." Wanda was Rachel's secretary. By asking Wanda to make the arrangements, she was hoping that the car rental company would not connect the dots that would lead to them selling the information about Lauralie's 'latest movement' to the media.

"That's a great idea," Anna agreed.

Just then, Lauralie's phone rang. She reached for her phone in her bag and glanced at the screen. It was Sebastian.

"It's my dad." Lauralie looked at both girls nervously. Anna and Rachel were as nervous as Lauralie, sitting on the edge of her bed. With the extensive media coverage of Colton and Lauralie, everyone would have learned about it. Unless, of course, if one was living up in the mountains or in some cave.

"Hi, Dad," Lauralie answered.

"Hi, sweetheart," Sebastian replied. "How's everything?" His voice filled with concern.

"You already know?" Lauralie sighed.

Sebastian chuckled. "I saw the pictures. Are you happy, sweetheart?"

"I am." A broad smile broke out on Lauralie's face. Anna and Rachel, who were watching her all this while, whispered between themselves and broke out in burst of giggles. They obviously knew where their conversation was headed.

"You'll have my blessing," Sebastian said. "I spent quite some time with Colton during his interview. I can tell he's a good man. In fact, a part of me had been hoping you two would get together." He laughed heartily.

"Colton will be happy to hear you say that." Lauralie glanced at the girls who were jumping up and down in excitement.

"I've already told him, I called him first. Had to make sure his intentions were in the right place, and that he knows what he's getting himself into. His feelings for you seem genuine, Lauralie." Lauralie was surprised and grateful that Sebastian had called

Colton. In his own little ways, Sebastian had always supported her endeavors. "I've got to go, Uncle Charles is waiting for me. Why don't you come up to the main house in the morning? I'll fix you breakfast."

After over two weeks away from home, she missed her father's pancakes. "That sounds great, Dad. I'll see you then."

"Your dad had given his approval?" Rachel asked in anticipation after Lauralie were off the line.

Lauralie nodded, and all of them squealed in excitement.

"Oh, Lauralie! You two are just perfect for each other," Anna screeched.

Lauralie wanted to believe her. She wanted to believe that there was nothing in the world that could break her and Colton apart. But a nagging feeling in her gut told her that the worst was far from over.

25

Two weeks had passed peacefully. Rumors had started to die down in the press. Members of the press were making up their own stories, but nothing particularly offensive. Whenever Lauralie and Colton met for dates, Lauralie would follow the false lead and car rental plans that had worked nicely.

Lauralie would pass the paparazzi stationed outside of her gate every morning in her Aston Martin. Once she was sure she wasn't being followed, she drove to Rachel's to retrieve her rented car, leaving her car tucked safely in Rachel's garage. And vice versa when she returned home every night.

Lauralie's doorbell rang when she was about to take a shower after she woke up. She glanced at the clock. Eight o'clock.

Who could it be at this early hour? Lauralie wondered.

Lauralie walked past the hallway, opened the door and there stood Anna, one hand clasping a newspaper, with a nervous expression. She glanced briefly around her, as if making sure there's nobody around, and pushed her way into the house without giving Lauralie a chance to speak.

"Anna, what's wrong?" Lauralie closed the door hastily behind her. Dread filled her stomach.

"Have you seen today's front-page news?" Anna looked at Lauralie with eyes about to pop out. Anna handed her the newspaper.

Lauralie shook her head and took the newspaper from her. Her hands were shaking badly. Sprawling across the front page was a huge headline that read *Celebutant's Boy Toy Lead Own Brother To Death*. Below the headline were several photographs of two teenage boys in Air Force uniforms. They were pictures of Colton and his brother. Lauralie read the report, which occupied the whole of the front page cover, in horror.

"Garbage! This is complete garbage!" Lauralie was on the brim of tears. What she feared most was that Colton had already read the newspaper. "This is reprehensible." Lauralie flung the newspaper onto the floor. "We'll sue. We have grounds. And then they'll have to print a retraction," Lauralie said desperately.

"We need to think carefully before we act." Anna paced up and down the living hall.

"This whole thing is just ridiculous!" Lauralie smirked. "Oh my, just look at the headlines!"

Just then, the phone rang and it made the girls jump. Lauralie glanced nervously at the phone. She knew who it was, if she guessed correctly. She picked up the phone carefully and muttered, "Colton?"

There was an eerie silence on the other end of the line, which confirmed Lauralie's guess. It was

Colton. And she knew he was upset. Very upset.

"Colton?" Lauralie called out again and glanced at Anna nervously. Anna was sitting on the sofa and had her hands clasped together as if she was praying.

"You've seen the news today, haven't you?" Colton's harsh tone startled her.

"Y.. Yes. I... I." Lauralie couldn't take it anymore. She sobbed. "I.. I am sorry," she mumbled.

Silence.

"We'll sue them and release a press statement," Lauralie continued, "saying that the report is untrue. Why don't we release the true incident? Once people read the true story, they'll see that you had nothing to do with Paul's death. And it may actually make you seem more sympathetic to the press."

"Sympathetic?" Colton snarled. "How about the part where they mention my sister's teen pregnancy, or call my niece a bastard? Or the paragraph that describes my parents as 'simplistic factory workers who accepted their lot in life'? How sympathetic is that? My god, I don't know what I'm going to say to my family."

"Colton, I'm sorry... I'm sorry." Lauralie sobbed. She tumbled onto the sofa next to Anna. Anna put her arm around Lauralie's shoulder and hugged her close as if to calm and comfort her.

"So, let me get this straight," Colton snapped. "My choices are to pose like a good little monkey and let the tabloids take my picture... My picture I don't mind, but to use a photo of my dead brother on the cover of their trash? Do you know how exploitative that is? Do you have any idea how my parents are going to feel when they see Paul's picture... his military picture? Oh my goodness!" he shouted.

"Colton, I know you're upset. But... but this isn't my fault." Lauralie cried.

"Of course this isn't your fault," Colton said condescendingly. "Nothing's ever your fault, Lauralie. It's all you know... you always have a great excuse to avoid any responsibility for what happens around you!"

"That's not fair!" Lauralie's sadness quickly turned to anger. "I didn't ask for my childhood anymore than you did. I can't help that photographers and reporters have stalked me since before I was even born!" she screamed.

Lauralie took a deep breath before speaking again. "Listen, I think we should take some time to calm down. We can talk things over after we've had some time to think."

"I don't need time to think, Lauralie," Colton said in a quiet tone. "I'm going to call my family and apologize for the fact that our entire family is being waylaid by the national media. And then I'm going to assure them that this will never happen again. I'm done, Lauralie."

Lauralie's world tumbled. Fresh flood of tears trickled down Lauralie's cheeks.

"Lauralie?" Colton paused. "You should also consider this my resignation." With that, Colton hung up the phone.

Lauralie clutched the phone tightly over her chest and sobbed loudly. Anna held her in her arms.

Lauralie didn't know what she was going to do, or how she would get him back. The only thing she was sure of was that she and Colton Dixon were far from finished.

A NOTE FROM THE AUTHOR

I'd like to thank my lovely readers again for your support. You guys rock! Without you, there would be no reason for me to keep writing these books. You're all wonderful and I so appreciate you from the bottom of my heart.

Follow the passionate story of Colton Dixon and Lauralie Shaw in *Stardoom Book 2*, due for release in March, 2016.

Connect with me on
https://www.facebook.com/sophiakingstonbooks/

And sign up for my **newsletter**

…..to get an email notification as soon as the next book is available. ***Don't miss a single installment of Sophia Kingston's captivating Stardoom series.***

ABOUT THE AUTHOR

Sophia Kingston is a writer of sweet romance, romantic suspense, chick lit and cozy books. She loves reading and writing since little and her short stories have been featured in local newspapers during her school days. She loves writing stories that will transport herself and the readers into another world.

At home, she plays a loving and faithful wife to a wonderful husband, who works very hard to support the family. What more can she ask for?

In her free time, you can find her reading novels and writing yet another story for her readers.

If you have enjoyed reading this book, please recommend it to your friends.

I always welcome your comments so connect with me on:

https://www.facebook.com/sophiakingstonbooks/

With lots of hugs!!

Printed in Great Britain
by Amazon